GLEAM FROM THE ABYSS

GLEAM FROM THE ABYSS

Shriraj More

For my family,

who taught me to see the world's hidden glow

"The fungi are the great recyclers of the earth, the interface
between life and death."

— Paul Stamets

"What we call the beginning is often the end. And to make an
end is to make a beginning."

— T.S. Eliot

Contents

Chapter 1: The Rain's Welcome

The rain came at dusk, as it always did on Nicobar Islands in April, a soft patter against the corrugated roof of the research shack. Aarya was sitting cross-legged, notebook on her lap and pencil shaking slightly in her hand. In three days since she had arrived, she had not written a word—not since the boatman, his face creased like old leather, had muttered something about *the ones who see in the dark* and left her there with a sack of rice and a warning to *stay close to shore*. The air smelled wet and earthy with a hint of something sharper, fungi-like, so that the island seemed to be claiming her, its peculiar scent perfuming her clothes.

There was little more to the hut than a box—naked wooden boards pieced together hastily, a desk that creaked on rusted hinges, a cot covered with a worn mosquito netting, and a kettle that wheezed at every lighting of the stove. Outside the jungle began abruptly and without any ceremony. A curtain of green, heavy with vines and banyan roots curled like serpents asleep—it was always breathing, always watching. She had journeyed only a few steps beyond the coconut grove, returning earlier each time, feet betraying her curiosity.

South Veyra was a name in a file, an outline on a satellite image. In person, it breathed differently. It did not welcome. It tolerated. It accepted her presence as one will tolerate a fly sitting on one's arm—unsightly but not worth swatting yet. The silence here was unlike any she had ever experienced. It was not a state of quiet but a state of waiting—of something unuttered, that rested just beyond the rustling of palm fronds.

At night, the light from her headlamp only made the dark darker. She saw eyes—not reflections, not glints, but a steadiness that signalled awareness. Not animal, not entirely. The island wasn't sleeping.

And neither was she.

The wind above South Veyra sneaked in off the sea like a rumour. It weaved and curled around the high-banked cliffs, it dragged fingers across the tops of the forest, and slipped through the half-cracked louver windows of the prefab lab where Aarya stood — barefoot, holding her breath.

Her skin itched again.

She leaned across the workbench, shoving a petri dish under the lens. The spore colony had tripled in size overnight. Fuzzy blooms were radiating outward in fractal, a brilliant cerulean in the low light. She blinked. The outer ring pulsed a little.

She didn't remember them glowing yesterday.

Behind her, the wall fan in the lab sputtered on. The solar panel had stored enough for use in the morning, but the reserve battery blinked red — on a loop. This island was never meant to be sustained or inhabited, let alone for field research. That was one of the reasons BioSynth insisted the work was to be unobtrusive. "Less interference, and more results," they'd said in their smooth, pre-recorded onboarding modules.

Aarya knew better.

Aarya took out the sachet of camphor Ma had given her, pressed into her palm the night before she took off from Kolkata. For the air, Ma had said. For memory. Camphor to cleanse, to remember, to protect.

Aarya lit it with the lab's emergency spark lighter, watching the flame flicker at the end of the bench. Smoke circled around her, for just a second obscuring the stink of salt and rot. It was idiotic. Sentimental. But this place--it altered her breath. It thickened her dreams. And the spores weren't just in the air anymore. They were listening, she sensed.

She unbuttoned her sleeve. The rash had escalated from the ushering trails it was before to swirls across her forearm, arranged in slow spirals, like the fungal colonies she had to map. A single bitter laugh coiled in her throat, forcing itself down.

How poetic, *Baba* would have called it. *The mycelium writes back.*

Outside, the jungle had awakened. A single black bird cawed three times from the canopy, then was silent.

And from the treeline, the flicker of two eyes-- still. Watching.

The winds had changed direction.

By lunchtime, above, the sky wore a translucent gray shawl, gauzy but vigilant. Aarya felt the drop in barometric pressure come in waves as she focused her field scope against a slatted window with panes streaked with salt from last night's tempest. Outside, the fungal colony she had tagged two days ago teetered shyly under its tarp—pearly caps veined in violet, sporing despite the saline zephyr. *It was as if the spores didn't care what tried to kill them, she thought. They would settle wherever the island would place them.*

She turned to the cot where her tablet blinked with a new alert:

"Subject 13-D exhibiting elevated spore count. Sample unstable. Decontam recommended".

The tag had come from somewhere within South Veyra's interior—the inner gorge there where the basin marsh edge carpeted the vertical rock with moss. That was three days ago. And the subject—a molted half shell the size of her palm— had been desiccated and cracked into silvery dust.

She started a voice memo.

*"**Note:** Pattern mismatch in sporulation timeline. Initial five-day latency estimate is incorrect. I will re-sample gorge perimeter. Possible vector interference?"*

In the room, her voice felt off, authoritative but remote. Like someone reading a diary they never wrote. She grabbed her scarf, the indigo one *Baba* brought back from Shantiniketan, and wrapped it tight. Outside the air had warmed, something thick and stifled, clinging to her skin like gauze. The horizon was blurry like it was wet ink. Seaward in the slope, the mangrove arms clawed at the sky like they were in slow motion.

Something rustled.

Not bird, not crab. It had a rhythm. A pause. A watching.

She froze mid-step and scanned the line between dune and treeline. The trees were dead, but somehow made it worse that they were dead.

Then all at once it was gone.

But the prickling behind her ears did not disappear.

Back at the shack the equipment pinged again. Another alert, and not from the tablet this time, a spore-meter, one of her custom hacks, flickered an orange pulse.

"Proximity sensor breach: 0.6 km NE."

Aarya furrowed her brow.

That was too close.

The meter's padlock ceased to flash its pulse. Aarya recorded her coordinates and replaced the meter into her bag, fingers grazing the edge of the fungal swab tubes next to the meter. Her breath was slow but shallow—as though her body would not allow itself to be calm.

She walked backward, keeping her eyes on the NE quadrant, toward the corner support post of the shack.

0.6 km. Mangrove rise.

That was near the inlet—where she'd first landed, what now seemed weeks ago but was only three days ago.

The memory surged like a tide.

The boat ride from Port Aurora had started so calm. Aarya had crouched mid-hull, her gearboxes lined with wet burlap to buffer any BioSynth sensors at outer stops.

As they left the port behind, the coast gently shifted: coconut fronds faded to tangled banyans, familiar shorelines melted into distanced, uninhabited quiet. She remembered her

bunkmate from the Institute calling it the Orphan Zone—
unmapped, unclaimed, unofficial.

The captain—a grandfatherishly old, silent Tamil man,
with tide-battered hands—did not ask questions. His eyes were
glassy and perhaps nearly blind, but his boat knew the route
better than any maps.

The fissures on his face like broken riverbeds.

The way he'd stared through her, when he'd called it:

"The ones who see in the dark."

He hadn't given time for questions. He hadn't even helped
to unload the boat. He just sat the bag of rice on the bank,
turned the bow around, and faded into the swell while
humming softly—half lullaby, half lament.

The motor took a last sputter like an expiring breath. And
she stood, barefooted in the surf, the hut a hundred paces away
on the sand, the jungle just beyond.

Aarya had studied the declassified British files in IICHA's
archive.

South Veyra did not fade in the memory.

It had been eliminated.

The deeper they pushed the more her breath tasted like
iodine and rust. The mangroves spread like the roots were
swollen into lungs. The fungi glimmered in canary yellow and
cobalt blue. There was one strain holding on to a partially
submerged branch, blinking - or nearly so, under the glare of
her monocle lens.

She'd felt it back then - before she'd stepped on the land.

Something pressing on the middle of her chest. Not fear, not quite.

A... presence.

As if the island had its own eyes. It knew she was on her way.

The boat did not dock that day.

She'd jumped from the boat, in the middle of the channel, cut-thigh-deep in brine, wading toward the shore with her bag hefted, muttering Ma's rationale like an invocation.

Observe first. Explain later.

That was Day Zero.

Now, she crouched beside the mangrove root near her little shack, inspecting the soil - soft, and the last-disturbance evidence. The scanner beeped quietly again. Then nothing.

The Gleamers were not making their presence known.

She had no delusions left.

She was not alone.

And if the spores could listen, then maybe someone else already knew what she had dragged out of the boat.

As Aarya was bent low over the muddy ground, the wet earth was turning to a mote in her eye instead, three days in and a dozen fungal logs in, Aarya saw something unsettling in the isle's damp soil. Her scarf—completely soaked from dew, stained by spores, was beginning to smell not just of her sadness and sweat, but also of the isle. Of rot and salt. Of soft decay. As if, in its own way, the isle was preparing her.

Claiming her.

The thought came without warning.

And so did the resonance of his voice.

"Stay right along the shore."

But Aarya was not along the shore anymore.

And the eyes—if they had seen her one time—they may not ever stop seeing.

She went back to the shack without documenting the infraction.

The tablet briefly waited for her on the desk, the cracked corner of its screen and flashing light like an unblinking eye. Aarya wiped her palms on her legs and tapped in her biometrics. She became stuck at the input field.

Observation Log - April 09, 2075 | 17:45 hrs
"Nothing moving. Fungal range acceptable. Humidity up. No anomalies."

Send.

A lie.

She started to prepare tea.

The old kettle had to fit right, just right, on the induction ring, a trick she figured out, the second day in. The steam hissing from the spout released thin, erratic threads of warmth that shadowed the shack in the smell of burnt coil and leaves made bitter by sunburn.

She sat cross-legged on the cot, her elbows resting on her knees and the steel cup in her hands. The tea was weak - mostly water with a few dry leaves in it, hot, and a habit.

Baba had made tea this way.

Every morning, in the small flat back in Shyambazar, right after he'd brushed the ants off his microscope tray, but before he'd opened the windows to let in the Hooghly air, he would hum while he waited-never a song, just a low sound, like he was tuning into something deeper. "A fungal signal," he used to joke. The underworld.

She could still hear that sound sometimes in the silence-between creaks of wood, in the lull after rain. She pressed the cup to her lips, closing her eyes.

But not now, the jungle wasn't quiet now.

It rustled-slowly, like someone was testing the weight of a step. Not wind. Not branches. An upright beat.

She opened her eyes.

There, outside the screen-covered window, was the glint again. Not light. Not reflection.

It blinked.

Once.

Twice.

And was gone.

She stood slowly, not spilling the tea, not moving to the door. She listened. Nothing followed. No approach. Just that stillness again-the breath-held hush she was coming to know.

The cup shook in her hand. The taste of the tea soured.

And then, without warning, the line returned-a sharp, full line in her mind:

"The ones who see in the dark."

Observation Log: April 9, 2075 | 18:30 IST

Subject: *Unnatural Bioluminescence & Eye Reflection in Vegetation Belt Theta*

"Faint reflective glint observed ~10m into grove. Stationary. Not animal-like. Will confirm with IR cam at 05:00 hrs. Unsettling frequency of 'pulsing' glow in Mycelial Bloom Cluster B."

The research shack had grown colder by night. Aarya wrapped her shawl tighter, ears tuned to the forest's strange silence. Not even the usual cicadas. Just the wind, and that low hum, intermittent, like breath through hollow bamboo.

She replayed the moment in her mind—those twin glints in the dark, just above ground level. Not eyes. Or not animal eyes. The reflection was too… slow. Deliberate.

With cautious steps, she reached for the packet of IICHA standard rations—compressed rice, rehydration salts, and a protein stick. Her stomach growled, but she didn't eat. Hunger seemed safer than distraction.

She sat back down, flipping to the back of her notebook. Doodles. Circles within circles. She hadn't realized she'd been sketching spores again—those luminous caps from Cluster B. They looked like eyes.

Aarya glanced toward the window, fogged and streaked with rain. Nothing outside but dripping ferns. And yet…

A sudden knock—soft, like a pebble tossed against the tin door.

She froze.

No one else was supposed to be on the island.

She rose, every movement calculated, and clicked the portable data unit to record audio. Then she stepped slowly toward the door.

Nothing. Just a gust of wind. The island playing tricks.

But when she returned to her notebook, something had changed.

The sketch on the page—

The circles within circles—

They were no longer spores. They looked like pupils.

The knock did not come again.

But Aarya's heart, traitorous and loud, refused to settle. She stood motionless for another minute, then peeled herself off the floor, knees trembling. The door creaked as she opened it—slowly, just enough to peer through the gap.

Nothing, only the rain, softening and pouring all at once, and the palm trees' silhouettes lurching above in the gloom.

She scuffled barefoot outside, the mud cool and slick against her bare feet. The grove beyond the shanty throbbed with mycelial luminescence, the bio-luminescent webs were burning, now flashing. It was as if the forest had veins - alive, alert, and listening.

Aarya scanned the clearing with her eyes. No footprints. No one in the brush. Just one thing was out of place: a small bundle, placed neatly on the wooden plank just off the door.

Wrapped in a palm frond, bound with jute fiber.

Cautiously, she picked it up and unwrapped it. Inside were three blue seed pods—moist, veined, delicate like lungs—and a folded square of paper. No words. Just a charcoal drawing: a hand, open. And within the palm, an eye.

Aarya's breath caught.

Not just the drawing. The seed pods—she recognized them from her training with the Biosynth Ecological Atlas. Veyraensis Indigo, a rare variant known to affect cognition and dream states. Indigenous groups used it ceremonially—but it had mild psychoactive properties when handled raw.

Someone was sending her a message. Or a challenge.

She took the bundle inside, placed it on her desk, and pulled the IICHA standard scanner from her satchel. The battery flickered, then powered on.

Observation Log 009-A | 9 April 2075 | South Veyra Island | 18:53 IST

"Received unsolicited biological samples. Unknown sender. Possibly local inhabitant.
Signs of intelligent placement. Visual symbol included—resembles panoptic glyph.
Will refrain from touching seeds until compound stability is confirmed."

She saved the log, locked the scanner, and leaned back. The rain's rhythm grew erratic—no longer gentle, but tapping like fingers, impatient and strange.

She glanced at the seed pods again.

Then at her notebook.

Those circles she had drawn. Not spores. Not coincidence.

They were eyes.

And just like the boatman had warned...

They were watching.

Inside the shack, the single coil bulb overhead gave off a soft buzz, casting long shadows across the room. The storm had not gone into full throttle yet, but she could feel it closing in on her—heavy in the air, curling like smoke at the edges of her nerves.

Aarya stepped over to the corner where the boatman had left a sack of rough rice and some dried turmeric root, salt, and a tin of dal, and a narrow bottle of mustard oil wrapped in newspaper. Nothing fancy, but enough. She poured a handful of rice into the steel vessel, filled it with rain-caught water from the collection drum, and set it on the small kerosene stove.

The flame took its time, coughing blue at first before settling into orange.

Her fingers, finally, began to relax with the ritual. Wash. Stir. Wait. Stir again.

She thought of Ma, as she always did when cooking. Even here, on a forsaken patch of fungal forest, the muscle memory came not from lab manuals, but her mother's quiet hands in their Shyambazar kitchen. Ma had taught her how to listen to rice—to hear it go from rattling like gravel to swelling, murmuring, as the steam worked its magic.

"The first scent of cooked rice tells you who you are," Ma used to say, tying her greying hair with a black ribbon.

"No matter where you go, beti, it brings you home."

Aarya closed her eyes and inhaled.

There it was. That smell—sweet, starchy, grounding.

Home.

She crushed a bit of dried turmeric with the bottom of her field knife and added it to the boiling dal. It bloomed gold. The smell mingled with the earthy scent of the rain, the fungal musk. An odd, comforting contrast.

She didn't cry, but something in her chest softened.

She missed the sound of the Rabindra Sangeet *Ma* played from her battered old phone, always crackling, always out of tune. Missed the overlapping voices from the neighbour's veranda, the hawker calls echoing down Amherst Street. She missed... Rohan, too. But that ache was buried deeper, wrapped in something unresolved.

She plated the food on the stainless-steel thali—one mound of rice, a ladle of turmeric dal. No pickle. No garnish. But warm.

As she sat on the floor cross-legged, the storm finally arrived in full—a curtain of wind and water, lashing at the tin roof. The shack creaked in protest.

She lifted a spoonful to her mouth. The dal had a burnt edge, but she welcomed the imperfection. It tasted like memory. Like survival. Like something real amidst everything that wasn't.

From outside, something howled.

Aarya didn't flinch this time. She took another bite.

She finished eating in silence. The rain fell in sheets now, drumming hard on the tin roof, rolling off in gutters along the shack's edge. The air smelled of wet ash and salt, and somewhere beneath that, the sharp green tinge of new fungal bloom.

Aarya rinsed the plate in collected rainwater, dried it with the edge of her shawl, and sat again at the worktable. The seed pods were still there, glistening faintly under the flickering light. She resisted the urge to touch them.

Instead, she opened her tablet and tapped into the IICHA soil-map overlay. Her fingers were steady, but her mind was drifting—threading together the patterns.

The grove where the footprints appeared yesterday. The cluster bloom she found with spores reacting to light. And now, these pods.

She drew a rough arc between the locations, and the points fell into an almost perfect crescent. Not a coincidence. Not natural.

"Not random decay. Not just rot. Someone—something—is arranging this."

Her head throbbed.

She leaned back, pressing the heel of her palm to her forehead. The fever had returned—dull, low-grade, but pulsing behind her eyes. It wasn't just the spores in the air. It was in her skin now. Her blood.

She checked her vitals on the wrist patch. Mild tachycardia. Slightly elevated core temperature. But within operable range. Technically, she was still field-capable.

Technically.

Another hum, this time from the northwest.

It was faint—barely audible over the rain. But not mechanical. Not like the drones. This one sounded human. A low vibration that rose and dipped, like a lullaby carried by the wind.

She stood again.

Opened the shack door slowly, letting the glow from inside fall across the mud.

The grove shimmered. Not just with spore-light now, but with something else.

Movement.

Just past the banyan line—where darkness should have swallowed all visibility—something shifted. A flicker of shadow. Two faint pinpoints of blue, almost imperceptible, like a night animal blinking from behind a leaf.

She didn't breathe. Didn't speak.

And in that stillness, the hum rose once more.

Not closer. Not louder.

But clearer.

A child's voice.

The last light faded behind the treeline and into the tangled wilds beyond, devoured by the thick canopy. Aarya lit the second stub of a wax candle, and the flame flickered against the air currents darting through the irregular seams of the corrugated shack. She huddled over a low table in the corner, her writing notebook propped open beside a glowing glass container of living bioluminescent lichen—her primary source of ambient light.

It was time for logging.

She dipped her pen into the ink bottle she had carefully refilled with carbon soot and water—Baba's old field trick— and began her field note:

Observation Log | 09 April 2075

Subject: Spore Bloom Patterns - Quadrant IV (Northern Grove)
Spore Density: 8.7/cm²

Morphology: Branched hyphal network expanding in radial symmetry. Pale green iridescence.
Odor: Slightly metallic, humid-earth undertones.
Additional Notes: Spore bodies appear active even in low humidity zones.
Hypothesis: Symbiotic adaptation to host fauna? Further sample analysis needed.

She paused mid-sentence, tapping the end of the pen against her chin. Through the slit of the shack's loosely bolted window, the grove lay in shadow, yet she could still hear it— soft rustles, a clicking chorus rising and falling like breath. The Gleamers? The idea struck her, unwanted and sharp.

That's when she noticed it. Just above the edge of her window: a flicker of movement.

She went still.

Not a drone. Drones were loud, blatant with their angular whines. This—this was quiet, measured. Like something watching. Or someone.

She felt her heart race in her chest when she turned her head to look away, as if reading the page. One hand cautiously inched down under the table for a small folding knife she kept taped beneath the table top. A metallic clink. Then silence.

Ten seconds passed. Then twenty.

Nothing.

Aarya exhaled, long and slow, and stood. It could've been a macaque. Or a vine's shadow caught in the flickering candlelight. Her mind was fraying faster than she liked to admit.

She blew out the candle and moved to the cot, wrapping the mosquito net low around her legs like a ritual. Her father had always said that the island's madness lived in the silences between thoughts. "Stay curious, but stay grounded," Baba had warned. "The moment you let fear write your thoughts, the forest will start answering them."

She shut her eyes and whispered aloud to the dark:

"I am not afraid of what watches. I am only here to see."

Somewhere in the black canopy, a faint gleam pulsed once. Then it vanished.

***

Chapter 2: The Weight of Duty

South Veyra Island | 10 April 2075 | 9:20 IST

The grove smelled different that morning. Damp, metallic, tinged with something sour—like fruit gone soft on the branch. Aarya paused at the edge of the trail, one boot sinking slightly into the mud, and checked the scanner. The reading blinked: $10.3/cm^2$.

She exhaled slowly.

The spores were multiplying faster than expected. The rate was outside IICHA's predicted growth curve—far outside. It should've prompted an immediate report.

But she said nothing.

She looked up instead. The trees here were taller, older, their canopies tangled with moss that shimmered faintly under morning mist. Clusters of spore sacs hung like lanterns, quivering in the humid breeze. As she stepped forward, one of them burst—softly, like a sigh—and released a glittering puff of green.

She didn't flinch.

Her body had begun to grow used to it. The tightness in her chest, the occasional heat behind her eyes, the dry edge to her cough—symptoms that had settled into routine.

The scanner chirped again. She adjusted the wavelength dial and swept the immediate area. That's when she saw them.

Footprints.

Two. One adult-sized. One unmistakably smaller.

Pressed gently into the wet earth, side by side.

Aarya crouched.

No tread. No drag. Barefoot.

The distance between the prints was wide—graceful, measured. Not the stagger of a lost tourist. Not even tribal.

No human settlements had been recorded here in over fifty years.

She pulled out her field camera and hesitated. Her hand hovered above the shutter button.

Log them.

That was the protocol.

"*Log all,*" Dey's voice had said.

Not *some.* Not *when convenient. All.*

But her hand didn't move.

Instead, she took out her personal notebook. The one not linked to IICHA's cloud. She sketched the prints. Lightly. Then smoothed the soil with her boot.

Gone.

Just like that.

The tablet on her hip vibrated. A new message.

Port Aurora Lab | Urgent Field Update

Re: BioSynth Drone Survey Deployment

"Surveillance unit 7-A scheduled to fly over South Veyra Grove Quadrants at 10:40 IST. Please ensure observation logs are complete and uploaded.
Log all findings. Visual confirmation of decay patterns expected.

— Dey."

Aarya stared at the message until the screen dimmed.

Then she stood up, pressed her notebook to her chest, and whispered to the trees:

"I didn't see anything."

The hum began again. Faint. Rhythmic. Like breath filtered through leaves.

10:28 IST

The sky above South Veyra had gone glassy—flat grey, sharp-edged, like a pane waiting to crack. Aarya stood under a thick-leafed palm, one boot wedged into the slope of a fern-choked incline, her tablet vibrating with an urgent sync alert.

Drone ETA: 12 minutes.

Upload Required: *Spore Metrics & Visual Confirmation.*

She looked down at the spore field just ahead—Cluster Delta. A sprawling patch of yellow-flecked caps, each about the size of a thumbprint. They were fresh, glistening, eerily symmetrical. She should have been cataloging each one.

Instead, she stared at the soil between the roots.

There had been more footprints.

Smaller this time. Only one.

Almost dancing.

She had erased them again. Quietly, with her field knife, pressing soil back into itself like smoothing out a secret.

Her head pulsed behind the eyes, a dull throb that swelled with each breath. She tasted iron at the back of her throat. The fever hadn't broken—it had taken root.

Aarya sank to a crouch, breathing through her scarf. She pressed the corner of the cloth to her lips and saw the faintest trace of blue-green when she pulled it away. Spore residue. Her blood, maybe. She couldn't tell anymore.

Her thoughts drifted—disobedient now.

Shyambazar, Kolkata | 2070

Kolkata. Bedroom curtain fluttering in the early evening breeze.

Ma standing by the stove, ash-stained fingers trembling as she held a folio of Baba's sketches.

Fungus spirals. Labeled species. Unclassified glyphs.

One drawing in particular—a set of eyes beneath a banyan tree. Beneath it, Baba had scrawled:

"They live where the forest remembers."

Aarya, just twenty-two, had tried to snatch the sketch from Ma's hands.

"These are just field notes, Ma!"

"No, they are not," Ma snapped. *"They're what killed him."*

The paper curled in the flames, and with it, something in *Ma* hardened.

From that day forward, everything Aarya brought home from the field—samples, printouts, even fungal stamps on her boots—was met with silence or scorn.

Now, in the silence of South Veyra, Aarya sat back against a stone and stared up.

A dark speck hovered against the cloudline, approaching from the northeast.

Drone Unit 7-A.

She had minutes. Maybe less.

She opened the tablet.

"Decay spread consistent with mapped patterns. No sign of ecological disruption or off-pattern formations. No anomalous footprints. No signs of fauna."

Attached photo: *Decay cluster. Contrast enhanced.*

She pressed **Send**.

The drone passed overhead with a sharp, chirping wail.

And the forest… stayed still.

11:10 IST

The drone was gone.

Its shrill whine had vanished behind the ridge line, leaving only the hush of dripping leaves and the soft clatter of distant branches shaken by its wake. Aarya stood motionless beneath the banyan archway where the soil had once cradled footprints—now smoothed out by her own boot.

Her hand, still holding the tablet, was slick with sweat.

She took one slow breath.

Then another.

Then she sat—right there on the mossy root, legs curled beneath her, the sun caught in threads through the trees. The ache behind her eyes ebbed slightly. The fever simmered low, like coals beneath skin.

Her throat burned. Not just from the sickness.

From holding it in.

The why of it all.

She pulled out her notebook. Not the official one. The soft, stained one she had kept since her field days in college. The one she never let Ma see.

She flipped to the back page. The glue there was still stiff from the old printout she had pasted—a copy of Baba's sketch, one she'd salvaged from a discarded scan. The spores had been drawn like mandalas, spiraling, intricate. He'd captioned it with a single line:

"Where rot is beautiful, life begins again."

She touched it now, the edge faded, the ink just slightly bled.

Shyambazar, Kolkata | 2070

"Don't keep his things," Ma had said the night she burned the folio.

"You're too much like him already."

She had watched the papers curl into themselves, corners catching flame like dry leaves in winter. *Baba*'s notations, his careful lines, vanishing in orange silence. Aarya had wanted to scream. But didn't.

Ma wasn't wrong.

Only incomplete.

She never understood that *Baba*'s madness wasn't about data or disease.

It was devotion. To mystery. To pattern. To life where no one thought to look.

And Aarya loved him for that.

Loved him more than she had ever been able to tell *Ma*.

Maybe that's why she'd taken the assignment.

Not just to study decay.

Not just to finish his work.

But to walk into the forest that he dreamed of.

And maybe—maybe—because *Ma* had tried to distance her.

And she couldn't forgive her for it.

South Veyra Island | 10 April 2075 | 11:22 IST

The wind shifted. A rustle came from the north.

Aarya tucked the notebook into her chest pocket. She rose, slow and steady, brushing moss from her knees.

"I'm still here, Baba," she whispered.

The forest gave no answer.

But somewhere above, a single leaf detached from the canopy and spiraled down—turning, softly, like something nodding yes.

18:40 IST

The wind outside howled against the shack's tin roof, a low growl rising with the sea's breath. Aarya had closed the windows tightly, yet the smell of brine and wet moss still crept in, as if the island itself refused to be shut out.

She hunched over her field notes, the lamplight flickering on the pages where her pen traced the outlines of spore clusters seen earlier. She labelled them "Cluster A4 – anomalous glow in twilight", then paused, eyes drifting to the small, sealed petri dishes set aside on the far end of the desk.

They pulsed faintly.

No external light source. No trick of reflection.

She leaned back in her chair and rubbed the bridge of her nose. Fatigue hung at the edge of her mind, as did a faint twinge of exhilaration. She hadn't imagined it. Whatever this bioluminescent response was—it wasn't normal.

Her datapad pinged.

New Message – IICHA Port Aurora

Subject: Drone Surveillance – BioSynth Units

Aarya,

Drone footage confirms multiple BioSynth pods operating near Site 9, South Ridge Sector. Proceed with caution. Do not engage. We are attempting remote interface but systems are firewall protected. More instructions to follow.

– Dr. Meghana Rao, Field Command, IICHA

She stared at the screen. BioSynth. So they were here.

She knew the Institute had suspicions about the private corp's activities—but this confirmed it. Unauthorized synthetic deployments on a biologically sensitive island. If the drones were collecting fungal samples... were they studying the same anomaly she was?

Her chest tightened. This wasn't just a field survey anymore. It was becoming something else—something her father would have pursued with the same obsessed glint in his eyes.

But she wasn't him.

Or was she?

She turned back to the glowing spores, shadows flickering across her face as the wind howled louder.

Inside the Shack | 10 April 2075 | 21:00 IST

She leaned forward and slid the petri dish into position beneath the handheld field scope. The bluish spores she had collected from Cluster A4 had arranged themselves into an unexpected pattern overnight—like a network, delicate and webbed, almost... intentional.

Aarya tapped the lens gently. Focused.

Under 60x magnification, the fungal hyphae looked like threads of glass, their ends sparking faintly—glowing without an energy source. She switched off the desk light and let the room fall into darkness. The spores pulsed again, soft blue and green, cycling every few seconds.

Bioluminescence wasn't rare.

But rhythmic bioluminescence?

That was something else.

She whispered into her recorder:

"Observation Log, Unofficial.

A4 specimen exhibiting light cycles of approximately seven seconds. No external stimulus applied. Spore density consistent with inland samples.

Note: Pattern resembles neural discharge rhythms. Unconfirmed."

She paused. Then added:

"It's... beautiful."

She sat in silence, watching the pulse continue.

A part of her wanted to reach out—to touch the edge of the colony with her fingertip. Baba would have. He never feared proximity. He believed in communion. That fungus could teach us something about interconnectedness—about memory itself.

Aarya hesitated. Then pulled on her nitrile gloves and gently opened the dish. She waved her hand near it, slowly. The spores flared brighter. She moved again. The glow responded.

Not just alive.

Aware.

Aarya sat back, stunned. The spores were reacting to movement. No airflow interference. No temperature fluctuation.

It was a response. A signal.

For a moment, all the weight—the fever in her chest, the silence from IICHA, the shadow of BioSynth—fell away. All that remained was this moment. Glowing threads. A mystery unfurling in the dark.

She stared at the pulsing spores, eyes wide.

"What are you trying to say?" she whispered.

22:47 IST

The spores pulsed quietly on the desk, a rhythmic blue glow tracing faint silhouettes across the shack walls. Aarya sat motionless, her gloved hands resting on either side of the dish. Her breath had synced with the cycle—inhale, glow. Exhale, dim. It was hypnotic. Beautiful.

Then—a thud.

Soft. Muffled. But unmistakably real.

It came from the left side of the shack—just outside the lab window.

Aarya's trance broke instantly. She blinked hard, as if surfacing from underwater, and turned toward the sound. Her body had tensed before her mind could register it. She stayed still, listening.

Nothing.

She waited.

Another sound.

Not a thud this time. A slow, wet dragging. Grass against wood. Like something brushing the side of the shack.

She stood quietly, careful not to bump the desk. Her hand reached for the field knife taped beneath the tabletop, tearing it loose with one firm tug. The weight of it steadied her.

She walked to the window—footsteps silent on the wooden floor—and peeled back the corner of the curtain.

Moonlight. Rain-slick grass. Palm shadows swaying.

No movement.

She scanned the left wall of the shack, where the dragging had come from. Then she looked down.

At the base of the wall, just inches from the window, something was resting.

A bundle.

Tied with jute, wrapped in what looked like fresh banana leaf.

Exactly like the one she found three days ago.

Except this time, something was carved into the outer layer.

A single, dark line drawn in sap—a spiral, thick and deliberate, ending in a small dot.

A fungal ring.

Or an eye.

She stepped back from the window slowly.

The spores behind her flared once. Bright.

Then dimmed.

And in the brief stillness that followed, the forest whispered—

Not with wind.

Not with water.

But with the soft, careful hum of a child.

She stared at the bundle from the other side of the window, her breath clouding the glass.

The spiral glistened in the rain—dark, organic, like it had been drawn with the sap of something living. It wasn't smeared. It hadn't run. Whoever had marked it had done so with precision.

And care.

Aarya's fingers curled tighter around the knife.

But she didn't feel fear.

She felt... chosen.

The wind rattled the corner of the shack as if to nudge her forward. She lowered the curtain and backed away from the window, her body taut with awareness. Every creak in the wood beneath her soles felt amplified. Every drop of water sliding down the tin roof echoed like a footstep.

She slipped into her poncho and stepped outside.

The rain had softened to a drizzle, the air heavy and lush. Jungle musk mixed with the metallic tang of wet earth. She crouched beside the bundle. The leaf wrapper was fresh, still warm from the body that had carried it. Or grown it.

She ran a gloved finger along the spiral. It stained her glove faintly.

It wasn't drawn. It was secreted.

She lifted the bundle carefully and brought it back inside, placing it gently on her worktable beside the softly glowing spores.

A small breath escaped her lips.

She peeled back the leaf.

Inside: three spore caps—one violet, one white, one pale green—and a flat square of what looked like bark paper. Hand-pressed. Fibrous. Natural.

There was no writing.

Only another mark: two concentric rings, each drawn by hand, the inner ring filled completely.

A glyph.

She scanned it with her tablet.

The software returned no match.

"Of course," she muttered. *"You're not in the system."*

She pressed record on her private log.

"Second unsolicited biological sample received. Left at northwest wall perimeter. Evidence of intentional placement. Organic pigment used for symbols. Fungal caps are not in IICHA database. Possibly new genotype."

She paused.

Then added:

"Or... someone doesn't want it catalogued."

She looked again at the spiral. It was not a warning. Not a trap.

It was a message.

And though the forest remained silent now, Aarya felt it—

She was being asked to listen.

23:11 IST

The bundle sat open. The spores pulsed faintly, as if breathing.

Aarya leaned closer, elbows on the table. Her fever hadn't returned, not fully—but something in her chest tugged downward, like her heart was trying to root.

She stared at the glyph—those two concentric circles, simple and ancient. Her lids fluttered. Her head dipped.

And the night unspooled into memory.

Kolkata | September 2072

Rohan's apartment, Gariahat. Dusk.

The fans spun slowly above them, scattering the scent of basil and rain. Outside, the windows were half-fogged from the humidity, vines curling in from the grill like gentle intruders.

Rohan stood barefoot in front of the shelf where his rescued ferns lived in tin cans and broken tea cups.

"They still fight," he whispered, stroking one frond with the back of his fingers. *"Even now, when we've taken so much. Humans choke them with heat."*

His voice cracked. Aarya lay on his bed—cool white sheets twisted around her, her skin flushed, hair damp from their bodies' closeness. Her fingers trailed the edge of his kurta.

"You still sound surprised," she murmured.

Rohan turned, eyes smoldering. The anger in him was not loud. It burned slow and low.

He crawled into the bed beside her, cupping her waist, pulling her close. His fingers were rough, earth-soaked.

"I need you," he breathed, his voice against her neck.

She arched into him. The room smelled of petrichor, sweat, and lemon balm. The vines swayed slightly—though the air was still.

"Then stay," she whispered. But even then, she knew he couldn't.

He was always leaving. Always pulled by oceans and oil spills, saltfields and protests. He was the storm, and she was the tether he never quite untied.

South Veyra | Present

Aarya blinked.

The memory left her mouth dry. The spores on the table shimmered, as if aware of what she'd just seen.

"*Feel this pulse,*" he'd said once, guiding her hand to a banyan trunk. "*They remember.*"

She reached for the pale green cap and held it near her cheek. Warm.

Something brushed the edge of her thoughts.

Not words. Not hallucination.

But something.

Something like breath.

Something like "*I need you.*"

23:42 IST

The spore bundle now rested in the ceramic bowl on her table. Aarya hadn't moved in minutes.

She was still—listening.

Outside, the forest trembled with nocturnal murmurings: a distant wingbeat, frogs in staccato bursts, a low rustle that didn't sound like wind.

And yet it was the silence inside her that hummed louder.

"*I need you,*" she heard again.

Only this time, it wasn't memory.

She rose suddenly. Not frantic—more like she was being pulled. Her boots thudded softly against the floor. She took the glass vial of spores, sealed it, and stepped out of the shack.

The jungle air hit her like breath against bare skin—warm, wet, familiar.

Her torchlight flickered, then steadied. She followed no trail.

Because something was guiding her.

The forest's edge | Minutes later

The clearing was faint, overgrown. The moon spilled its silver reluctantly between dense canopies.

Aarya crouched near a low thicket, pushing leaves apart. Something glinted—faintly bioluminescent. It was another fungal bloom.

But this one…

She leaned in.

The caps were translucent, like skin stretched thin. Underneath, they pulsed in synchrony. Her fingers trembled.

Gleamers, she thought.

They found me first.

She reached for her recorder—but her hand froze.

Because a shape stood just beyond the clearing.

Still. Watching.

A shadow with shoulders. Human-like. But the eyes—

—they glowed.

Not fully luminous.

Not mechanical.

Just...shining, like some forgotten instinct, like tapetum lucidum reflecting moonlight.

And then—

"*Aarya?*"

Not loud. Not animal.

But human.

And heartbreakingly familiar.

Her blood surged.

"*Rohan?*" she whispered, voice cracking.

The shape didn't answer.

It just turned.

And slowly, deliberately, walked back into the trees.

She ran.

Not fast—not out of fear—but with a kind of reverence. Each step felt tethered to a thread that might snap if she hesitated. Her boots crushed moss and leaves, the jungle closing behind her as quickly as it opened.

"*Rohan.*"

She whispered it again, not as a call but a prayer.

The shape ahead stayed just beyond reach. Never turning. Never rushing.

Just... leading.

Branches caught her sleeves. She didn't flinch. Her torchbeam darted between roots and vines, until the battery died, swallowing her in shadow.

She didn't stop.

This can't be real.

But it didn't matter.

Because grief never plays fair with reason. And neither does love.

A narrow gorge, deeper in the forest

The figure paused again—near a collapsed tree trunk, half-covered in mushrooms. Their caps glowed faintly blue, spilling ghost-light upward.

Aarya skidded to a stop, breath short, heart rioting.

"If it's you," she gasped, *"just… don't vanish."*

The figure turned halfway. Not fully. A profile at most. Hair tangled. Shoulders hunched. And those eyes—still faintly shining. Less unnatural now. More…

Familiar.

Like something remembered in a dream you weren't sure you ever had.

"You used to say," Aarya choked, *"that plants listened. That they could hear us breathe."*

A pause.

And then, a low voice—distant but unmistakable:

"They still do."

She broke.

Tears welled, caught in the humid air. Her knees trembled. Her body remembered everything his voice carried—earth, rain, and the unbearable comfort of being known.

"Rohan…" she whispered.

But the figure turned again—slowly—and stepped behind the trunk, vanishing like mist.

She ran to the spot.

Only to find…

Nothing.

Just the soft rustle of ferns and the luminous curve of fungi.

She stumbles into a clearing swallowed by moonlight, breath ragged, chest heaving. Ferns part, their silver fronds recoiling like they remember her. And there—where the jungle's breath thickens, where the fungal haze lifts like mist—something stands.

Not a figure. Not entirely. A shape, tall, still, tinged with a familiar weight.

Aarya's breath hitches.

It doesn't speak. It doesn't need to.

There's a flicker—a shift of shoulders, a tilt of head, the particular gravity of knowing her.

"Rohan?"

The name cracks through her like lightning. The air doesn't echo it. No reply comes.

But the jungle hushes.

The shape remains. It neither beckons nor retreats. Its presence is a question drawn in fog.

Her skin prickles with sweat and memory. Her fingers reach—tremble—don't quite touch.

Around her, spores drift like snow, some glowing faintly blue, some dissolving before her eyes. She blinks, and for a moment, it looks like he's smiling.

Was that ever real? Or is the forest learning her grief, mimicking it back to her in the shape she most wants to hold?

She takes one step closer.

The shape leans into shadow.

Another step.

Nothing. Just silence. And spores. And vines that curl upward as if listening.

She stands there for a long time, heartbeat slowing, watching the shimmer where he—it?—stood. Or still stands. Or never stood at all.

Somewhere in the distance, a fungal pod exhales. A bird calls once, then twice.

Aarya doesn't turn away.

Not yet.

Not until the shimmer fades.

She stood in the clearing, hands slack at her sides, pulse still hammering from the chase. The humidity pressed down on her like water, beading along her brow, slipping down her back.

It felt real.

His voice. His gait. Even the slight turn of his shoulder.

Rohan had always walked like the ground whispered secrets to him.

She looked around again.

Still nothing.

No footprints in the soft mud. No path through the underbrush. Just the shimmer of dew and the blue-capped fungi lining the trunk where the figure had vanished.

Aarya stepped forward, crouched, and touched the moss.

It was warm.

"*Not imagined,*" she whispered to herself. "*Not completely.*"

Something caught the corner of her eye—tucked between the roots.

A folded piece of cloth.

She reached for it slowly. It was damp, fraying at the edges. A torn piece of off-white khadi cotton, the kind Rohan always wore. There was something scribbled in ink, bleeding slightly from the moisture.

She held it under her torchlight.

One line, in Rohan's handwriting:

"*Trust the spiral.*"

Her breath hitched.

Is this another hallucination?

She pressed the cloth to her chest, closing her eyes. The forest pulsed gently around her. The spores in the grove ahead shimmered, then stilled.

She stood.

Behind her, the wind stirred through the canopy—soft, almost melodic.

And for the briefest moment, she felt it again.

Not presence.

Not a shadow.

But a hand brushing her wrist.

When she turned, no one was there.

Only the jungle, swaying. Watching.

The cloth in her hand was still damp when she reached the shack.

Aarya shut the door behind her with more care than usual, as though the forest might still be listening. Her breath came shallow; her boots left a trail of wet across the wooden floor.

She sat down slowly at the desk.

The spores in the petri dish had dimmed while she was gone. Or maybe her eyes were adjusting. The night had a way of taking color and turning it in on itself.

She laid the cloth flat on the table.

The ink was still there: Trust the spiral.

"Trust," she echoed, voice thin.

She turned on her tablet.

The screen flickered—mud-speckled, faintly cracked from the earlier chase. It glowed with the sterile blue of the IICHA interface. She blinked at the prompt:

New Observation Log: 11 April 2075
Please confirm location + sample description.

Her fingers hovered above the keys.

She should log the bundle. The cloth. The glyph. The whisper.

But she couldn't. Not tonight.

Her body ached. Her temples throbbed. The hum, though distant, still trembled at the edge of perception. And beneath all that, Rohan's voice—its warmth still braided through her spine.

She began typing.

Cluster A4 spore colony stable. Luminescence irregular. Field status: Normal. No anomalies to report.

She read the line twice. Then, a third time.

And hit **Save**.

It was her second omission in as many days.

But it no longer felt like defiance.

It felt like preservation.

She leaned back in her chair, one hand pressed to her forehead. Her skin was damp. The pressure behind her eyes had returned—hotter now, less like a headache and more like heat pressing outward.

She whispered to herself:

"Just fever. That's all."

The shack creaked gently in the wind.

The spores pulsed once—then again. Quicker now. Almost flickering. She turned to look at them and, for a split second, saw a shape in their rhythm.

A spiral.

Her eyes widened.

The glyph on the cloth. The fungal rings near the grove. Her father's sketch.

All spirals.

A sudden wave of dizziness washed over her. The world tilted slightly left, then fell back into place. Her hand slipped from the chair arm. The edge of her vision grew soft, vignetted.

She reached for the water bottle, missed.

Her head slumped forward onto the desk.

Outside, the wind shifted. The hum returned.

Not above. Not beyond.

But beneath the floorboards.

It was slower now. Clearer. A melody, simple and haunting.

A child's voice.

"*They still do,*" Rohan's voice whispered again.

She lift her head.

The spores on her desk pulsed once. Then again. Erratic now. The walls of the shack pulsed with the hum.

Aarya wiped sweat from her brow. Her fever had not returned, but a strange heat clung to her—low, persistent. She stood slowly, the floorboards creaking beneath her bare feet.

She crossed to the window and unlatched it.

The forest was still.

Then—movement.

Not a Gleamer. Not yet.

Just a flicker—light brushing between two trees.

She narrowed her eyes.

It was... glowing.

A spore trail?

A signal?

Whatever it was, it moved again.

And this time, Aarya didn't hesitate.

She grabbed her scarf, her small field kit, and stepped outside—into the night-shimmered air, into the hush that follows fever, into something calling her back to the grove.

The spores pulsed once more on the desk behind her.

Then dimmed.

***

Chapter 3: Womb of the Island

The grove on Veyra Island exhaled a damp breath, heavy with earth's musk and a faint, acrid tang, like fruit gone soft. Aarya's boots sank into the mud. Vines draped ancient trunks, their leaves slick under a sky still bruised from rain. Spores floated, light as chalk dust from her mother's classroom, catching the faint glow of her tablet's shield. Beyond, BioSynth drones whirred, their chirps sharp against a deeper hum—a child's note, soft, threading through the trees, stirring her fevered thoughts.

A cough tore through Aarya, harsh, unrelenting. Her skin burned, spore-sickness rooting deeper. She steadied herself against a tree, its bark biting her palm, and glanced at her tablet. The log blinked: Decay patterns. Dr. Dey's letter loomed—*Report all, no exceptions*—its weight like the data probes she'd once calibrated under his stern eye. Yet Anjana's words, gentle, pressed back: *Trust your heart.* Aarya's fingers trembled, caught between duty's pull and the hums urging her onward.

She crouched, tracing a spore trail in the mud, its glow weaving *Kolam*-like curls. *Ma* surfaced in her mind—Kolkata, 2066, rain hammering a school gate's rusty overhang. Aarya, thirteen, had eyed the flooded lane, eager for friends. *Ma's* hand caught her, firm, her wet sari clinging as she snapped, *"Water takes, stay close."* Her voice, sharp with a social science teacher's knowledge, wove tales of Bengal's floods, but at home that night, she'd turned to Math, her true gift. Over a chipped table, *Ma* had sketched equations—runoff rates, precise to two decimals—her chalk flying, eyes alight. "*Numbers shield,*" she'd said, making Aarya count till the sums sang. Now, Aarya tallied spores—ten per square centimeter—*Ma*'s clarity guiding her to type routine observation, burying the footprints she'd found: one adult, one child's, etched deep.

The hum rose again, a child's murmur, faint against the drones' pulse. Aarya's chest ached, fever and memory entwining. Her father, *Baba*, Kolkata, 2067, stirring dawn tea— three spoons clinking, a raga humming. "*See their dance?*" he'd asked, tilting a microscope to reveal a spore's glow, his pen noting observations. Aarya, nineteen, had memorized tea, song, sketch, her awe kindled. Now, the grove's sheen echoed his slides, and she erased anomaly detected, her lie a nod to his fungi's life, *Ma*'s sums anchoring her count.

A vine grazed her wrist, cool as a whisper, and Rohan flickered in her mind. Kolkata, 2072, his room at dusk, ferns crowding the sills. "*They still fight,*" he'd said, tracing a leaf, his voice bitter at warming's choke. His touch was slow, warm, his breath soft—"*I need you.*" Aarya had melted into sheets, his scent—soil, rain—her haven. Now, fever climbing, the grove's vines pulsed like his plants, her longing sharp.

She typed—"*Soil stable.*"

Another secret kept, honoring his earth, guarding the hums from sterile labs.

The drones' chirps tightened, closing in. Aarya pressed deeper, vision wavering, following the spore trail's glow. Anjana's voice emerged—Kolkata, 2073, lab dusk, cardamom steam curling from her mug. "*Hide what sings,*" she'd murmured, nodding at a slide's flicker, her bangle soft against the bench. Aarya had cleared pulse noted then, Anjana's warmth her guide. Now, the grove's hums called, and her tablet stayed blank, empathy outshining Dey's command.

Her knees faltered, the fever heavy, but the trail shone, daring her to see. More footprints—small, certain—curled by a root. *Ma* again, 2070, Kolkata's tram stop, her grip steady in the crowd's buzz. "*Strangers hide harm*," she'd warned, her jasmine oil sharp, recounting city unrest. At home, she'd taught Math—crowd flows, probabilities—her pencil swift, making Aarya solve till patterns bloomed. Now, Aarya counted hums—four seconds apart—*Ma*'s logic shielding what moved unseen.

The grove's murmurs swelled, the child's hum weaving with the drones' threat. Aarya's strength gave, her tablet slipping into mud. *Baba*'s sketches, Rohan's ferns, *Ma*'s sums— they held her. No labs, her vow, and routine observation her defiance, tying her to the hums' pulse. As darkness claimed her, the spore trail glowed, alive, its song unbroken.

The hums grew bolder, a child's soft cadence weaving through the grove's damp air, tugging Aarya deeper into the tangle of vines and shadows. Her tablet's glow cast faint light on the spore trail, its *Kolam*-like swirls gleaming like the chalk patterns *Ma* once drew on their Kolkata kitchen floor. Aarya's cough rattled, the fever tightening its grip, but she pressed on, each step a defiance of Dr. Dey's cold directive—Log all, no mercy. Anjana's whisper lingered, softer, warmer: Let them breathe. The words steadied her, a counterpoint to the BioSynth drones' sharpening chirps, circling closer.

She paused by a gnarled root, where the mud held footprints—small, deliberate, beside an adult's heavier tread. Her heart quickened. The hums felt alive, not just sound but presence, daring her to look beyond the tablet's sterile grid. She typed soil stable, her fingers trembling, the lie a shield for what moved unseen. Anjana's face flashed—Kolkata, 2074, her rooftop, chili-sharp mango pickle shared under a starlit sky.

"*Let them breathe*," Anjana had said, her dupatta grazing Aarya's arm, speaking of Nicobar's lost tribes, erased by logs like Dey's. Aarya had left her tablet blank that night, Anjana's laugh a spark. Now, the grove's glow echoed that pause, urging silence over betrayal.

A vine curled against her ankle, its touch damp, and Rohan surfaced—Sundarbans, his hand firm through mangroves. "*Feel this pulse,*" he'd said, tracing fungi, his voice cracking at warming's ruin. Later, in his room, his touch fierce, mud on their skin— "*We're theirs.*" Aarya had clung to him, counting breaths, missing him now as the fever burned. The grove's pulse matched his, and she erased trail noted, honoring his earth, her longing a quiet vow to guard the hums.

The drones' chirps spiked, mechanical, relentless. Aarya's vision blurred, but she knelt, counting spores—eight per square centimeter—*Ma*'s numbers grounding her. Kolkata, 2070, a tram stop's clamor, *Ma*'s grip tight in the crowd. "*Strangers hide harm,*" she'd warned, jasmine oil sharp, her social science tales of unrest cloaking fear. At home, she'd taught Math, her pencil dancing—crowd flows, probabilities—until Aarya saw patterns bloom. Now, those sums held firm, guiding her to log routine observation, hiding the footprints' truth.

Her knees wavered, the fever pulling, but the spore trail shone brighter, a dare to venture deeper. *Ma* again— their balcony, lantern light flickering. "*Night buries risks,*" *Ma* had murmured, her shawl slipping, weaving Andaman's tribal losses into warnings. Her hand, heavy on Aarya's shoulder, kept her close. The grove's quiet now mirrored that night, its hums a secret Aarya cradled, her tablet slipping as darkness loomed, the glow alive, unbroken.

The grove's air thickened, a cloying mix of wet bark and spores that clung to Aarya's throat. Her cough scraped, each breath a labor as the fever carved deeper. The spore trail pulsed ahead, its glow weaving through roots like the *Kolam Ma* etched on festival mornings, faint but unyielding. The child's hum lingered, soft as a lullaby, curling around the BioSynth drones' staccato chirps—closer now, slicing the jungle's murmur. Aarya's tablet trembled in her grip, its log open, cursor flashing like a warning. Routine observation, she'd written before, but the trail's dare held her, urging one last lie.

She sank to her knees, mud cool against her palms, and traced the footprints again—small toes, an adult's heel, pressed deep as secrets. Anjana's voice broke through—Port Aurora, 2074, the jetty's salt-heavy air, waves crashing below. *"Keep their secrets,"* Anjana had said, sketching coral, her pencil scratching *Kolam*-like curls. Her gaze, fierce yet kind, had steadied Aarya's hand as she cleared sheen detected. Now, the grove's hums echoed that whisper, and Aarya typed no activity, her heart racing, shielding what lived beyond Dey's reach.

A leaf brushed her cheek, damp, stirring *Baba*—Kolkata, his lab at dawn, tea spoons clinking, raga soft. *"See their dance?"* he'd asked, a spore's glow alive under his lens. Aarya, nineteen, had watched, awed, her world his wink. Counting spores now—seven per square centimeter—she saw the spore dance in the trail's sheen, her lie a vow to his fungi's pulse, *Ma*'s numbers steadying her tally.

Her vision frayed, the fever a tide pulling her under. The spore trail blazed, daring her to follow, but her strength broke. She slumped against a trunk, tablet slipping, its glow faint in the mud. The hums sang on, alive, a child's note threading through her fade. Anjana's secrets, *Baba*'s sketches, *Ma*'s sums—they bound her to this defiance, her last no activity a shield for the unseen, as darkness swallowed her whole.

Mud swallowed Aarya's tablet, its glow snuffed like a candle's last flicker. Her body slumped, fever a heavy tide dragging her under, the grove's pulse thudding in her ears. Spores settled on her skin, soft as ash, their *Kolam* swirls blurring into shadows. The child's hum lingered, a thread woven through the air, unbroken despite the BioSynth drones' shrill whine—close now, their lights stabbing through the canopy's weave. Her breath hitched, shallow, as the jungle claimed her weight.

A faint raga stirred, *Baba*'s dawn hum, Kolkata, his tea spoon clinking thrice. His wink her sun. The memory frayed, fever stealing its edges, leaving only the groove's glow, alive like his slides. A chalk snap broke through—*Ma*, at home, her Math swift, Kolkata, sketching arcs of floodwater on a slate. "*Numbers shield,*" she'd said, her eyes fierce, teaching Aarya to count till the world held firm. That clarity dissolved now, spores her only sum, their count lost in the haze.

Cardamom drifted, faint—Anjana, Kolkata's lab dusk, her mug steaming. "*Hide what sings,*" she'd urged, her bangle's clink a vow. Aarya's hand twitched, empty, the tablet gone, but her heart clung to that song—the hums, not hers to betray. The drones' chirps sharpened, mechanical, circling the tree where she lay, mud cradling her like Hooghly silt. The hums held, a child's note, faint but sure, pulsing beyond her fading sight.

Vines brushed her arm, cool, final. No more logs, no routine observation—only the grove's breath, heavy with secrets. Her vow, no labs, burned through the fever, tying her to the unseen, to footprints she'd never name. The hums sang on, alive, as darkness folded her in, drones hovering, their lights unanswered.

The grove's hums softened, a child's note thinning, barely threading through the drones' faint whine—distant now, or lost in her fade. Aarya's fingers twitched, no tablet to hold, only mud's slick weight. Anjana drifted—Port Aurora's jetty, salt on her sketch. "*Keep their secrets,*" Anjana'd said, her pencil tracing coral. That vow held now, Aarya's no labs a shield for the unseen, like *Ma*'s fire for *Baba*'s ghosts. Her cough slowed, counting breaths—*Ma*'s sums, four seconds apart—fading into silt-dark quiet.

Spores settled, light as ash on her skin, the grove a shadow of that sickroom's glow. *Baba*'s last cough, *Ma*'s burning hands, the hums—they wove her defiance, guarding footprints she'd never name. Her mind sank deeper, haze folding over, the child's hum a final thread, unanswered, alive.

Aarya drifted, her mind unmoored, the grove's damp weight easing into a softer haze. Mud no longer clung; instead, a breeze carried the scent of jasmine and marigold, warm, alive. She stood in a courtyard, stone tiles smooth underfoot, a house unfolding around her—whitewashed walls, wooden shutters ajar, sunlight spilling through. Rohan was there, his laugh low, tending a garden where hibiscus flared red, orchids bowed purple, and frangipani gleamed like stars. Sunlight kissed the leaves, exotic ferns curling at the edges, their corners gold in the morning's glow.

The child's hum faded, a distant echo, swallowed by the rustle of petals. Aarya reached for a flower, her fingers grazing velvet, but the fever's pull lingered, blurring the garden's lines. *Ma*'s voice flickered— her chalk tapping a slate at home, Math's rhythm steady. "*Numbers hold truth,*" she'd said, her sums mapping floodwater's dance, teaching Aarya to find order in chaos. Now, those counts slipped away, only the garden's pulse remaining, its flowers swaying as if counting breaths.

Baba stirred, faint, his lab's dawn, a spore's glow under glass. His raga threading through tea's steam. The memory dissolved, leaving only the courtyard's light, orchids alive like his fungi, no microscope needed. A shadow passed—drones, perhaps, their whine dulled, or just clouds crossing the sun. The house held firm, Rohan's hand brushing hers, his scent of earth grounding her drift.

The drones' whine was gone, or too faint to pierce the courtyard's hush. Flowers trembled, hibiscus folding into lotus, sunlight spilling like water. Rohan's gaze met hers, earth on his hands, and the grove's hums vanished, leaving only the garden's breath, soft, unbroken.

The courtyard's warmth held Aarya, its tiles still radiating the day's heat, though the sun had dipped low, casting long shadows from jasmine and hibiscus. The house stood quiet, its ochre walls soft in the dusk, the last guest's laughter fading beyond the gate. *Griha-Pravesh* was done—vermilion smudged on the threshold, rice grains scattered, their blessings lingering like pollen. Aarya stood in a *sari*, crimson silk woven with gold, its pleats brushing her ankles, heavy yet alive against her skin. Rohan faced her, his cream kurta crisp, *dhoti* folded neatly, his eyes catching the lantern's glow, warm as earth after rain.

No hums reached her now, the grove's childlike notes silenced in this haze, no drones to pierce the stillness. Aarya stepped closer, the *sari's* border grazing a lotus petal floating in the stone basin, its surface rippling. Rohan's hand found hers, fingers threading slow, deliberate, pulling her into the house's open hall. The air carried sandalwood, faint from the morning's *puja*, and she felt the fever's weight lift, her body light, unbound.

A memory flickered—2074, Kolkata, Rohan's room, dusk, his breath on her neck. "*I need you,*" he'd whispered, ferns at the window, their love slow, woven with longing. Now, he drew her near, his palm warm against her waist, the kurta's fabric soft under her touch. She leaned into him, her cheek brushing his, the *sari*'s gold threads glinting as they moved to the courtyard's edge, where hibiscus burned red in fading light. His lips found hers, tender, then fierce, a rhythm older than the grove's pulse, their shadows merging on the tiles.

Ma's voice slipped through, faint—2070, Kolkata, her chalk mapping sums at home. "*Numbers bind us,*" she'd said, her Math a quiet shield, teaching Aarya to hold fast. That order dissolved here, only Rohan's heartbeat counting time, her vow, no labs, a silent thread tying her to lives unseen. The jasmine trembled, petals falling, and Aarya sank into his arms, the house theirs alone, its walls guarding their fire.

Aarya's chest slowed, the haze deepening. The garden shimmered, hibiscus bleeding into frangipani, sunlight pooling like spilled ink. Her vow, no labs, pulsed once, faint, tied to the unseen—footprints, hums, lives not hers to name. The courtyard faded, its flowers folding into dark, the breeze gone, only a single hum lingering, soft, unanswered.

The darkness tightened, pulling Aarya back from the courtyard's fading glow. Mud clung to her cheek, cold and slick, the grove's damp breath pressing against her skin. Her pulse thudded, slow, uneven, as if counting the seconds between the child's hums—four, maybe five, a rhythm *Ma* would've charted. Spores settled in her hair, their faint sheen catching a stray beam from the drones, now distant, their chirps muffled by the canopy's weave. Her fingers twitched, reaching for the tablet, but it lay buried, swallowed by the earth like a secret too heavy to hold.

A cough broke the quiet, sharp, scraping her throat raw. The fever burned hotter, a tide dragging her thoughts to Kolkata, *Baba*'s sickroom, where camphor hung thick and dust coated the air. Arun Sen lay shrunken, his biologist's hands sketching air, *Kolam*-like fungi alive in his fevered eyes. Aarya, sixteen, had stood frozen at the door, watching *Ma*—Paromita—gather his sketches, her *sari* taut, face carved with fear. One night, *Ma* fed them to a clay pot's flame, ash curling bitter as Hooghly silt. *"They took him from us,"* she'd said, her voice low, shielding Aarya from their pull. Now, in the grove, Aarya's lie—no activity—burned like that fire, guarding the hums as *Ma* had guarded her.

The child's note stirred again, thin but stubborn, weaving through the grove's pulse. Aarya's breath hitched, her mind slipping to Anjana—Port Aurora, March 2074, the jetty's salt-heavy air, waves crashing below. Anjana leaned close, hair damp, sketching coral, her pencil tracing *Kolam*-like curls. *"Keep their secrets,"* she'd said, nodding to the sea, her gaze fierce yet kind. Aarya's tablet had blinked sheen detected from a reef sample, but Anjana's hand brushed hers, urging silence. She'd cleared the log, heart racing, Anjana's smile quick as dawn. Now, the spore trail's glow echoed that jetty, and Aarya's empty hands vowed silence again, Anjana's whisper a shield against the drones' circling threat.

Vines curled against her arm, their touch damp, stirring Rohan—Sundarbans, 2073, his hand firm through mangroves. *"Feel this pulse,"* he'd said, tracing fungi, his voice cracking at warming's ruin. Later, in his room, his touch fierce, mud on their skin—"*We're theirs.*" Aarya had clung to him, counting breaths, missing him now as fever carved deeper. The grove's pulse matched his, and her vow—no labs—hardened, honoring his earth, her longing a thread tying her to the hums' unseen lives.

Her vision blurred, the spore trail dimming, but *Ma* surfaced— their balcony, lantern light flickering. Her hand, heavy on Aarya's shoulder, kept her close, jasmine oil sharp. Aarya had felt her care, if heavy, bats chirping, *Kolam*-like shadows on tiles. Now, those shadows danced in the grove, and Aarya's defiance held, her count—seven spores per square centimeter—*Ma*'s logic shielding what moved unseen, her tablet gone, but the vow alive.

The grove's darkness pulsed, a heavy shroud that smothered the courtyard's fading light. Mud pressed against Aarya's cheek, its chill seeping into her bones, her breath shallow, ragged, as fever burned through her core. The child's hum lingered, a faint thread weaving through the jungle's damp breath, barely audible over the distant whine of BioSynth drones, their lights now faint pinpricks in the canopy's weave. Her fingers twitched, clawing at the earth, searching for the tablet long swallowed by the mire. Spores dusted her skin, their glow dim, like embers scattered from a fire she could no longer see.

A cough tore through her, sharp as a blade, doubling her over in the mud. The fever dragged her mind to Kolkata, 2070, *Baba*'s sickroom, where camphor stung the air and dust clung to a cracked ceiling. *Baba* lay frail, his hands tracing air, Fungi alive in his fevered gaze. "They live," he'd whispered, spores his final song. Aarya, sixteen, had watched *Ma*—Paromita— burn his sketches one night, ash curling bitter as Hooghly silt, her voice low: "They took him from us." That fire had been

Ma's shield, guarding Aarya from his obsession. Now, Aarya's lie—no activity—burned brighter, a vow to protect the hums, mirroring *Ma*'s fierce love.

Vines brushed her arm, damp and cool, stirring Rohan—Sundarbans, his grip steady through mangroves, tracing fungi. "Feel this pulse," he'd said, voice cracking at warming's ruin. In his room later, his touch fierce, mud on their skin—"We're theirs." Aarya had clung to him, counting breaths, her longing now a knife as fever surged. The grove's pulse echoed his, and her no labs vow hardened, tying her to the hums, to lives unseen, just as she'd held his earth close.

The child's hum grew bolder, a soft cadence cutting through the haze. Aarya's vision wavered. Now, the spore trail's faint glow recalled that jetty, and Aarya's empty hands honored that vow, shielding the Gleamers from BioSynth's reach.

Her knees sank deeper into mud, strength ebbing, but *Ma*'s voice anchored her, their balcony, lantern flickering. "Night buries risks," *Ma* had murmured, shawl slipping, her tales of Andaman's lost tribes cloaking fear. Her hand, heavy with jasmine oil, held Aarya close, bats chirping, *Kolam*-like shadows on tiles. That care, heavy yet warm, lived now in Aarya's count—seven spores per square centimeter—*Ma*'s sums hiding what moved in the dark, her tablet gone, her defiance alive.

The hum swelled, closer, and shadows shifted. Aarya's eyes fluttered, catching glints—eyes, gleaming like fireflies, amber-green in a child's small face, jade in a woman's steady gaze, silver-gray in a man's wary stare. The child, wiry, teak-skinned, crouched near, vine-woven hair brushing her bark skirt, hums soft as a lullaby. The woman, ebony skin taut, leaf-woven hair framing jade eyes, knelt, her bark wrap rustling, hands gentle. The man, sinewy, weathered, his coiled hair tied, loincloth stark, gripped a bone knife, his silver-gray eyes sharp, hissing low—words Aarya couldn't grasp, fear of her presence clear. The woman's hum countered, calming, her touch cool on Aarya's brow.

Early Morning | 03:20 IST

Darkness surged, then cracked. Aarya stirred, mud still beneath her, but softer, a woven mat now cradling her. The fever's grip loosened, her breath easier, though haze clung. She blinked, finding the child beside her, amber-green eyes glowing softly, a faint hum on her lips. The woman sat close, jade eyes steady, her hands folding leaves, a salve's tang in the air. The man was gone, his absence heavy, but the hums wrapped Aarya, warm, alive, trust flickering like a spark in the gloom.

Aarya stirred, her body heavy, soaked in sweat, as if the fever had wrung her out like a limp washcloth, and left her weak and fragile. She was on a woven mat, the dried fronds were rough to the touch, in a hidden niche in the Veyra Island grove. It was a sacred pocket of air, still, canopied with trees so large, gnarled, and grey that they had formed a vaulted ceiling, shrouded in a dappled dimness that was flecked with spores that were being released by fungi. Vines hung low, their leaves shining, and the ground breathed like a living being, smelling of moss and rot yet holy. Her breath was laboured and thin, but the embers in her chest had gone cold, except for the compelling tremor of tension underneath.

Next to her was a child, appearing no older than six, squatting low, her skin dark teak, catching just the hint of refracted light in the cracks of the canopy, gleamed slick like polished wood. Her eyes shimmered ochre-green, like fireflies vibrating in the moonlight, rising and flickering as she blinked. Her gaze, full of the instant wisdom of a momentary dream, was full of knowledge. The child was narrow framed, lean, svelte like a sapling of the jungle with faint ribs showing through her taught skin. Her short coiled hair burst tightly, trapped away with thin vines with bits of flesh hanging like tentacles, a single bead of dried amber sap. A skirt of woven bark camouflaged from her waist down, and lent lashes hung purposefully from the edges. She hummed an unsettling tune, swayed and hummed softly, muted and strange, vibrating through the hollow chamber, creating a wave of warmth flaring through dizziness. She rested her small hands on her knees, only delicate little fingers that resembled small twigs, chipped talons pointed and smeared with dirt.

The woman, in her thirties, sat closer, her presence serene, a steady anchor. Her ebony skin, taut and unblemished, shimmered faintly, as if kissed by the grove's damp breath. Her eyes glowed deep jade, their light soft but piercing, like sunlight through a forest pool, holding Aarya's gaze with unspoken care. Her face was angular, cheekbones high, lips full, set in a calm line. Her hair, close-cropped and coiled, was threaded with dried leaves—broad, waxy, green fading to gold—woven tight, framing her brow like a crown. A bark cloth wrap clung to her lean, muscular frame, knotted at one shoulder, leaving her arms bare, sinews flexing as she pressed a gentle hand to Aarya's wrist, her touch cool, deliberate. A woven satchel hung at her waist, bulging with unseen tools, its fibers dyed with streaks of ochre and ash. Her posture was poised, legs folded, bare feet dusted with soil, toes curling into the mat.

Somewhere across the depression, a man stood, thirty-five, his weathered face as rough as bark, scarred lightly along his arms, etched by years of the jungle. His eyes burned silver-gray, their glint sharp, like moon on steel, narrowed with suspicion, dancing as they settled on Aarya. His body was sinewy, broad-shouldered, designed for stealth, every movement tight, controlled, like a waiting hunt. His own hair, thick and tightly coiled, was tied back by a cord made of twisted vine, hanging down past his neck, a solitary bone bead flashing at the tip. A loincloth made of bark cloth, fringed and worn, was low on his hips, held in place by a cord with a bone knife, blade chipped but sharp, clenched in his hand. His knuckles turned white, veins standing out against his skin, and a growling low in his chest came a string of words lost to Aarya but full of warning. His stance was tense, one foot advanced, toes digging into the ground as if he stood prepared to lunge or run.

The child's hum grew softer, threading through the hollow, a melody that seemed to hold the grove's pulse. Aarya's pulse steadied, her gaze drifting from the child's amber glow to the woman's jade calm, then to the man's silver-gray edge. The woman's fingers tightened slightly, grounding her, while the man's knife caught a stray beam, its glint a silent challenge. Aarya sought to speak, but her throat flared with embers, silencing her voice. A cough broke free, then another, each a jagged plea, and the child drew nearer, her hum deepening into a resonant cadence— It was not a lullaby. It was older than that. Woven not for solace but to bear a weight unspoken. The woman lifted a hand, palm open to the air, then rested it softly upon her own heart, a gesture poised in the liminal space between greeting and parting, delicate as a leaf's fall. In that brief moment, with fever's blaze still burning in her blood, Aarya felt the soft sprout of faith, vulnerable yet deep, sprouting in the sacred soil. The hideout whispered around them—leaves trembling, spores falling, murmurs vibrant—its holiness embracing Aarya, frail but reviving, with an exquisite hope.

The woman did not talk. Neither did anyone else. Yet Aarya sensed language all around her, unexpressed but abundant - in sidelong glances, silences, or just in the way the child's murmuring changed when Aarya stirred.

Aarya wanted to get up but her body felt stuck. It was as though the fever had anchored her to the mat. She became hyper-vigilant about her body and how her skin felt wet with sweat and grime. The pain in her arms and legs was not just from walking too much, it felt deep, ancestral. It felt like fatigue from simply being an outsider or foreigner.

The man remained standing, proud like a knife. His breath was scant, shoulders tight and it seemed her awakening had set off a number of calculations within him. His body had plenty of scars, some long faded and very old, others fresh and lighter, irregular like the lines created by lichen on a tree. He was only wearing a rough loincloth. Around one wrist was some kind of twirled band with sinew and fiber from tree bark and the other wrist was empty, bare other than an undistinguishable patch where something was formally.

He said something then—not to Aarya, to the woman. One word, sharp and heavy. She used the same restraint in her demeanour. Her tone sounded low, fluid, and unhurried. Aarya couldn't place the language, but the sound reached her as a sound of the wind or rustling of dry leaves. Something authentic to the island.

The child had found a perch closer. She sat cross-legged now, a hand loosely placed on Aarya's forearm. Her touch was tinged with leaves in the wind - grounding and airy. The brightness in her eyes didn't fade, but Aarya noticed a flicker - like a change in candlelight when someone steps into the room.

For the first time, Aarya thought about her appearance to them. Her shirt wet with sweat, the ripped sleeve. The bruised knee from her fall near the mushroom trail. The chain looped around her neck, still clinging onto just a single silver ring— Rohan's. The otherness of her was impossible to ignore.

She glanced back to the woman. They shared a glance, a gaze.

There was no anger in those jade eyes. No fear. Only intention, and something else. Some kind of grief, perhaps. Or recollection.

Aarya closed her eyes again, not, she thought, from weakness, but something closer to surrender. Not capitulation. Not abandonment. Just quiet surrender—to the hums, to the damp cradle of the grove, to the presence of these beings, who did not even have names in her mind yet but already had taken root in her body's awareness.

She succumbed to the fever once more and as she did, the humming intensified; it was as if the very earth under her was beginning to exhale.

She had no idea how long she had slept. It had loosened its hold. The grove held no clocks; no bells, no markers of order. Only the gentle path of light across leaves, the annular direction of shadows on bark.

Her body felt like her body again, though it felt weak, like an old cup, once cracked, now glued back together. She shifted slightly, and the sound of the frond mat was enough to pull presence.

The woman was still there.

She had not moved far, only provided space, not distance. She was sat on a low, rounded stone, smoothing the edge of a long folded leaf with a fingertip. The action was so domestic, so banal it caused a tightness to rise behind Aarya's eyes. Reminders of kitchens and folded laundry and the women lives lived when no one looks.

"I-"

Her voice startled herself. So dry. So hollow. The syllable was unmoored before it could turn into word.

The woman looked up.

Aarya made another attempt: *"Thank you."* She gently tapped her breast. *"Aarya."*

The woman neither repeated the sound nor offered her name in reply. Instead, she paused for a moment at the Aarya's glance, gave a small nod that was slow and thought out, then looked down to the earth and traced her finger in the soil. A line. Then an arc. A spiral. A shape Aarya recalled, not a letter, not a number, but a glyph. Something primeval.

The woman laid her palm beside it. Looked at her. Waited.

Aarya engaged in the same gesture—hand on earth, fingers trembling with sensations.

Somewhere in distance, the man clicked his tongue against his teeth, an almost reptilian sound. Aarya turned slightly and saw he still clutched a knife edge. His cautiousness was still intact and wild.

Even so, he did not move closer. He allowed the moment.

And then the girl returned—coming from behind a low thicket carrying a gourd shaped like a bowl. She moved with instinctual poise, as if she were learning the way of the earth beneath her feet.

Without a word she came to Aarya and knelt. She held the bowl with both hands; in it some warmth, some fragrance—smoke curling upwards from the bowl—nothing more than a hint of root and seed, smoke and soil.

The glow of the girl's look flickered—amber-green strands of light, like a dawn fire behind clouds—then, as if responding to a thought that Aarya had not voiced, the girls' mouth smiled.

Not wide. Not opened. A slight lift of the corner of the mouth.

And Aarya, still not knowing where the actual of dream ended and the meaning began, accepted the bowl with both hands.

The bowl felt warm in her hands. It was almost too warm. She held it delicately, steadying her breath. The liquid was thick and murky, a deep ochre base mixed with something darker—ground bark or seed, Aarya thought. Tiny green flecks floated atop the liquid like crushed leaves. The smell began to rise—earthy, nutty, foreign.

Aarya waited and glanced at the child, half-expecting for the child to nod or motion and break the silence. But the child waited, still watching. Still humming, but barely now, like the timbre of a sound waning on the edge of memory.

Aarya brought the bowl to her lips.

The first taste was bitter, then sour, then something else, something like the coolness of mint, like mint crushed in clay, and then a rolling heat, slowly, that settled behind her throat. It was not unpleasant. It was medicinal. It was alive.

She drank the liquid in small sips, pausing between each one. Her body reacted far faster than her mind. And the fever, previously coiled deep in her belly, began to unspool like the slow tide rolling back. Her skin cooled. Her breath deepened. The stiffness nestled behind her eyes softened.

When she was finished, she held the bowl back out to the child. The child took it without a word and padded away, disappearing within the vines without a sound.

Aarya leaned back heavily against a wall of woven canopy, feeling the tug of exhaustion upon her again; not the sharp fevered type of exhaustion, but the peaceful kind when healing is starting. Aarya found the woman again.

Watching her now, quietly, and without fear. Her face was angled and refined—high cheek bones, her wide eyes shimmering in that strange, jade light. She had small, raised scars on her shoulders; equal and opposite scars, like ritual markings. Her hair—a tight coiled braid, entwined with broad, flat leaves—was more of a crown than ornamentation, it seemed sacred. She looked young and ancient.

She looked, Aarya thought, like someone who had never left this forest. Not just in years, in generations.

The woman rose unhurriedly and walked toward Aarya— not rushing, nor was she reticent. She knelt in front of Aarya and placed her palm again, for just a second, on Aarya's chest, on her heart. It was not investigatory or clinical, but oddly felt like permission.

Then she reached into a pouch on her hip, and pulled out a smooth, oval seed. No bigger than a fingertip, it was polished until shiny, and glowed faintly, like it might be sleeping something inside it.

She carefully placed it into Aarya's palm, wrapped her fingers around it, and murmured a word—just the one. Soft and foreign. Then she turned towards the path away from Aarya, leaving her alone in the twilight hush of the grove, the hum of the forest still awake around her.

The woman had disappeared. The grove fell back into silence, so complete it seemed woven from the forest itself. Aarya lay still, curled around the seed, which now pulsed a faint glow—like the afterglow of a forgotten lantern. Rain dwindled in tendrils down. Through the green hush and over the earth, the sound of water was almost memory.

She closed her eyes—and the past opened, quietly, like a window.

Shyambazar, Kolkata | 2057

She was nine. Shyambazar. The flat above the sweet shop where they lived then was old, dented wooden shutters, and yellowing, flaking walls. Water gleamed from the eaves like a line of silver. The lanes below were muddied with ankle-depth water, and the power was out again. The smells of boiled rice and fried green chillies drew into their home from the kitchen. Aarya burned with fever, skin blazing like a griddle, and breathing frantic. Paromita sat next to her on the iron-framed bed, drenched from the rain she had run through to get crushed tulsi leaves from the neighbor. She wrung out a cotton gamchha, soaked with cold water, and placed it on Aarya's brows.

"Ei rokom jhore toh city-o bhenge poreshow," she whispered to herself more than to Aarya. "This kind of rain breaks the city."

A creaky ceiling fan. Wet pages of the Anandabazar Patrika lying sprawled on the armchair. In the other room, her fathers voice crackled through the news broadcast. He was mumbling about policies, sounding frazzled.

"This Sinha is a dream seller," Baba spat, turning the volume up. *"Yash Sinha thinks reparations will save us. Save whom? These fishermen in Canning? The shopkeepers in Behala who are once again underwater? And now there is another 'Solar Soveignity Fund'- what a joke."*

Paromita did not look up. She dipped the cloth again, pressed it to Aarya's temple. "Better a dream than bulldozers," she said steady. *"R.K. Vardhan would destroy the entire east bank and turn it into a 'smart corridor' if he could have his way. You want a climate-proofed mall in Khidirpur?"*

"He's practical," Baba said, intervening now, his hair tousled from worry. *"He speaks of security, not fantasies. How long do we wait for global pity to arrive?"*

"Not pity," Paromita clarified in a controlled tone. *"Responsibility."*

Aarya shifted slightly beneath the sheet, half-listening. With the haze of fever still clinging to her, she felt their tension—two flows of tide in opposing directions. Sinha, the prime minister, and his climate tribunals and community grants. Vardhan, the opposition hawk who spoke like a builder, with his eyes on GDP projection lines and drone views of the disaster zones.

She opened her eyes just a bit. Saw her mother as a shadow. Saw her father as arms crossed tight. Saw the candle flicker in the wind from the slats of the shuttered window.

"*All I want,*" Paromita whispered, not much louder than the rain, "*is for her to come round without burning.*"

And she had. In time.

South Veyra Island | 11 April 2075 | 04:28 IST

But even now, years later, the hush returned, as they stood under a canopy well away from home. The hush between downpour and recovery.

Aarya blinked.

The grove filtered back through the fissures of her memory—first the smell of damp bark and ash, the moss-cold touch beneath her, then the dull hum, low and constant, like a lullaby remembered badly. She shifted her weight slightly. The seed had stopped glowing. It sat quietly in her palm now, like a stone.

She raised her head.

The sky above looked more green than blue, hidden behind a net of interlocking leaves, the kind that let the light in slivers. Somewhere, the forest was exhaling—rain falling not in drops, but in whispers. A soft hissing, like wind rubbing through reed. For a moment, she wasn't sure she had actually imagined it—all of it. Paromita's voice, the apartment in Shyambazar, her father's restless pacing. The room and its arguments had receded like a tide and left her here, in this strange grove.

And then—movement. A small hand brushed her shoulder, like a feather. Aarya turned slowly.

The child stood there. Watching.

She provided almost no sound—bare feet clean of mud, breath nearly non-existent. On her shoulder, her hair coiled like vines. Teak-brown skin shone around the edges of the glistening humidity, with subtle traces of ash or pollen. A necklace of thorns encircled her neck like a crown, and a skirt flared out like damp fabric shaped into petals.

But it was her eyes—amber-green, glowing even in the shadows—when Aarya lost her breath. The eyes shimmered. Not like eyes lit up by light, but like coals burning below. A still gleam, steady, knowing, and decidedly not innocent.

The girl lightly pressed two fingers against Aarya's wrist and then placed her palm over Aarya's chest, right where her fever still glimmered.

Aarya tried to speak—her tongue was thick, and her throat was dry. "I... *where am I?*" Aarya croaked, sounding strange even to herself.

The girl said nothing. She began to hum.

Low and breathy, the sound slipped underneath Aarya's skin. It felt like something old and gentle - like lullabies in a language she didn't understand, like palm fronds making noise above tram wires, like the sound the wind made as it threw itself around the corners in Shyambazar after a storm.

Aarya could feel her body settling back into itself.

Somewhere behind the trees, the female gleamer's shadow stirred again. But still she did not return - at least not yet.

The child did not leave. The child stayed, still one hand pressed against Aarya's chest, the other cupping the now dark seed in Aarya's palm, as though to remind her: it matters still. You are still held. You are still here.

For the first time since she had collapsed in the grove, Aarya felt the fever's edge recede. Not gone - but receding. Like the tide that had once washed over the lanes of Shyambazar, fading back into memory.

Shyambazar's monsoon dwindled into the warm earth below her limbs...

She wasn't in her childhood bed anymore.

The damp of the forest gently pressed into her back, cool now, not fever-hot. For a moment, her breath stopped. A lull—just like how it feels in the haze between dream and waking. She heard it again: the hum. Not like the floating, soaked in Rabindra Sangeet and eucalyptus vapor, from Paromita's throat, but more primal. Older.

She turned her head, slowly, like she still belonged more to a time past than a present.

There he was.

The child.

The very same who had been around in the haze before— a sylvan creature in a body of flesh if she hadn't felt his touch. He was crouched next to her now, small knees painted with dust, fingers holding a bowl of bark. His eyes glowed softly, amber-green, like a fire-fly more or less contained in human form. He regarded her—not as prey, not as a foreign body, but with a serious curiosity that would make her throat ache.

His hum was softer this time. A variety of sound circling around the moment.

Aarya blinked. She felt her limbs stuck. But not bound.

The child offered the bowl and held it with two hands, cupped, the way her mother offered her warm rice porridge. Not with authority. With invitation.

Aarya's fingers shook when she accepted it. The bark felt like warmth to her, in some way. Like it had life.

She didn't say anything.

There was no need.

The child tilted his head and smiled, just a flicker, perhaps unsure if this world could allow it. Then, he reached out with his small hand and feather-light, touched her forehead. Right where Ma had laid the cloth.

The hum shifted. One note lower. Steady. Reassuring.

Aarya exhaled.

She was no longer lost.

Not to fever.

Not to memory.

Not to the forest.

The child sat by her, legs tucked beneath his bark skirts and luminous moss. And for a time, they simply breathed together.

***

Chapter 4: Hands of Care

The world returned slowly—like breath drawn through wet cloth.

Aarya lay on something softer than mud but denser than memory. Her fingers curled against woven reeds, the mat faintly damp beneath her palms. The ache in her chest had dulled, and the heat behind her eyes was gone, replaced by a strange lightness. Not comfort. Not yet. But absence. The fever had receded.

She blinked.

The ceiling above her was not a ceiling at all—but canopy. Thick green woven with bone-white driftwood and broad, cured leaves. Morning light filtered through its seams in fractured gold. A few spores still floated in the air, drifting slowly, glowing faintly blue as they passed through a sunbeam.

Beside her, the child sat cross-legged, chin resting on her knees. She was watching Aarya without blinking, lips parted just slightly. A low hum pulsed from her throat—steady, quiet, more vibration than sound. It trembled against the air like breath against glass.

Aarya shifted. Her body felt hollowed, light, but intact.

The child reached forward, unafraid, and pressed something cool and fragrant to Aarya's temple. A poultice— leaf-wrapped, slick with sap, smelling of crushed roots and smoke.

Aarya caught her breath.

The child's eyes—amber and green—glowed faintly in the shaded light. Not unnaturally. Just... fully. As if they'd never needed electricity to see.

A rustle. The woman entered.

Her footsteps were soft, even on packed soil. She moved with quiet precision—spine long, arms graceful, a bundle of dried sporecaps in one hand. Her hair was plaited with vines. Her gaze found Aarya immediately.

Jade.

Her eyes were jade.

She knelt by the firepit, humming low, and began grinding something between two stones.

Aarya tried to speak. Only air came.

The woman looked up. She didn't smile. But she didn't turn away either.

Instead, she dipped her fingers into the salve and gently pressed it to Aarya's collarbone—where the rash from the fever had once flared red and angry.

The touch was careful. Cool. Measured.

Not clinical.

Not transactional.

It was the kind of touch Aarya hadn't felt in years—one that asked for nothing but recognition. Not data. Not diagnosis.

The hum continued. Low, harmonic. The child's voice now joined by the woman's—two tones layered, soft as mist.

A resonance passed through Aarya's skin, not just heard but felt, like a second heartbeat stitched beneath her own.

She swallowed.

Something inside her—wound tight for weeks—unclenched.

And just like that, she realized:

She was not alone.

She was being kept.

Not imprisoned. Not studied.

Kept.

05:19 IST

Aarya's fingers traced the edge of the poultice, already losing its coolness to her skin. The woman's hands moved with ritual precision—sorting herbs, folding leaves, crushing dry caps with a stone polished smooth by time.

She wasn't a nurse. Not a scientist.

Not tribal. Not wild.

She was something else—someone shaped by knowing, not naming.

Aarya's mind began to stir. Quietly. Professionally.

No visible lesions on the woman's hands. No calluses. No scars.

Tendon movement—fluid. Grip strength, controlled. Pulse rate steady. Respiratory rhythm unlabored.

Then the child shifted, dragging her index finger along the soil beside her. Aarya noticed the way her nail gleamed—translucent, almost crystalline at the tip. She scratched herself deliberately on a thorn. Just a nick.

The blood that welled was dark, nearly violet.

Not thick. Not runny.

It sat like a jewel for a heartbeat—then disappeared. Sealed shut. Not a trace left.

Aarya's breath caught.

No inflammation. No swelling. No platelet film. No clotting response as understood by human hemostasis. This is not immunity. This is sovereignty.

She turned her head slowly.

The child was watching her again.

And smiling.

Before she could respond, a rustle broke the edge of the clearing. Firmer footsteps this time. Heavier.

The woman's movements paused.

The child's hum fell silent.

A shadow passed across the open wall of the shelter.

He stepped forward.

Taller than the others. Shoulders broader. His skin darker, hair braided close to the scalp with bone-white twine. His chest moved with each breath like he'd been climbing. His jaw set, unmoving.

And his eyes—unlike the others—did not glow.

But they watched.

And they remembered.

05:43 IST

The male did not speak.

He didn't need to.

The moment he stepped into the shelter's edge, the air shifted. The hums faded. The child stilled, her eyes flicking between him and the woman. The woman rose, not startled—but aware. Her shoulders squared without tension.

A quiet negotiation unfolded without words.

The male's eyes moved from the salve bowl to Aarya.

To the child.

Back to Aarya.

His jaw worked once. Then settled.

He doesn't want me here, Aarya realized.

Not just because I'm a stranger. But because I've brought something he can't yet name.

She held his gaze.

No malice. But weight.

The kind of weight old trees carry before they fall.

He spoke—not to her, but to the woman. Low syllables, short and rhythmic, like fragments of a lost language. Not quite speech. Not song.

The woman replied in tone alone. One hum, lower than before, followed by a sharp exhale. Her hand rested briefly on the child's head.

The child, still watching Aarya, took her hand and placed it flat against her own chest.

Aarya felt it: the heartbeat.

Slow. Steady. Resonant with something she couldn't measure.

The male saw it.

And stepped back.

Not in surrender. Not in acceptance. But as one who understood a line had been crossed—and chose, for now, not to draw blood.

He disappeared into the trees without sound.

The hums did not return.

Only the soft rustling of leaves overhead.

Aarya exhaled for the first time in minutes. She glanced down at her hand. It still held the faint scent of the poultice.

She didn't know if she was welcome.

But she wasn't unwelcome either.

And sometimes, that was the beginning.

The trees had grown quiet.

Not silent—but listening.

Aarya sat by the low firepit as the woman tended to the herbs. The child curled near her, tracing loops in the dirt with a twig—spirals again, imperfect but repeating. The pattern moved inward, always inward.

The poultice on Aarya's skin had dried. Her fever was gone, but something remained—a thrum, low in her chest. As if part of her had aligned with something outside herself. A frequency, a rhythm.

The spores overhead pulsed once.

She looked up.

And paused.

There—just above the tree line—a thin shimmer, nearly invisible. A flick of light, like the afterglow of an insect wing or the faintest arc of reflected glass. It moved. Then stilled.

Her stomach turned.

Not because it was unnatural.

But because it was too familiar.

She stood carefully, eyes narrowing. Walked out from under the grove's canopy and into the open fringe. She stared at the sky. Nothing but mist and high cloud.

But she knew what it was.

A drone. Cloaked.

Likely BioSynth's. Possibly not.

She reached slowly for the data patch on her wrist. A faint blue pulse confirmed it: uplink detected. A brief handshake with a server node. No data exchanged yet.

Not yet.

She returned to the grove. Her eyes met the woman's.

The woman was already watching.

No fear. No surprise.

Just... recognition.

As if she had seen it all before.

06:36 IST

The uplink blinked again—stronger this time.

Aarya stepped away from the clearing's edge and ducked under the canopy. She tapped the screen on her wrist. A secure notification expanded across the tablet interface.

PRIORITY MESSAGE — IICHA FIELD INTEL

"Multiple heat signatures confirm drone activity in Ridge Sector.

Suspected PLA origin.

South Veyra quadrant mapped via satellite proxy—Loop Sweep 96A.

Upload pending flora-fauna anomaly reports by 1600 IST.

— Port Aurora Command"

She stared at the text.

PLA origin.

Chinese drones.

Even out here, under trees older than time, the ghosts of politics came circling back.

Her pulse rose. She didn't move.

Then—something cracked open inside her memory.

Port Aurora Lab | 29 March 2075 | 17:10 IST

Rain beat hard on the corrugated roof. Inside the lab, everything smelled of phenol, solder, and soaked paper.

The map glowed on the wall—South Veyra's spines rendered in gradient blue. A dotted path curved across the northern ridge.

Dr. Meghana Rao leaned toward it, stylus in hand.

"That's PLA flight path—confirmed twice this quarter. Not satellite-grade. Low-altitude drones, cloaked. They're not scouting weather."

Anjana didn't look up from her tablet.

"PLA's got holdings in half the agri-bio corps in Asia…"

The words echoed as Aarya stared at the notification on her tablet, fingers frozen above the keys.

She remembered how the air in the lab had gone still after Anjana said it.

Singapore proxy fund.

Chinese-controlled.

A third of BioSynth.

Not on paper. Not in headlines. But real. Present.
Embedded like spores beneath bark.

"Nobody wants to call it out," Anjana had muttered.

"Too many elections. Too much money."

Dr. Meghana had folded her arms then, her gaze hard on
the map.

*"Same tactics, different century. They came through Bengal in 1967
with Mao's blessing. 'China's Chairman is our Chairman'—remember
that one? They bled our borders red for a revolution they didn't have to
fight."*

"And now?" Aarya had asked, quietly.

"Now they want to own the blood itself."

12 April 2075 | 07:05 IST

She blinked back into the present. The jungle leaned closer, the
tablet screen pale against the green.

Upload pending flora-fauna anomaly reports by 1600 IST.

— Port Aurora Command

Aarya's mouth was dry. She tapped the tablet's edge,
forcing the alert to minimize. The battery dropped by 3% in
the process. One drone. Maybe two. Sweeping the eastern

ridge—where the fungal bloom was thickest. Where the Gleamers lived unseen.

And now, tracked.

Not for safety.

For sequencing.

She looked up—and found the woman watching her. From across the firepit. Eyes steady, not accusing. But understanding.

As if the past Aarya had just remembered... the woman had never forgotten.

She sat for a long time beside the firepit.

The woman resumed folding the dried sporecaps, weaving them into palm threads. The child pressed a spiral into the earth with a curved stick, one loop after another, never quite perfect but always complete.

The drone hum had faded, but its ghost lingered in her ears.

Aarya tapped the tablet once more. The screen flared to life, clinical, detached.

Pending Log Entry: South Veyra — Flora-Fauna Survey
Observation Date: 12 April 2075
Anomaly field detected: YES / NO
Upload spore activity, blood chemistry, and biome shift logs.

Her fingers hovered.

The child looked up.

Not expectantly. Not afraid.

Just... knowing.

Like she had already seen what Aarya would do.

"Their blood itself."

Anjana's voice. Meghana's silence. China's stake in the green corporation wearing India's flag.

The spirals. The hums. The healing. The gaze of the male Gleamer.

Aarya sat straighter.

Her throat was dry, but her hands were steady now—steadier than they had been in days. She knew what she was doing. What it meant.

And what it risked.

She tapped the tablet.

Anomaly report: NEGATIVE

Fungal systems within range. No anomalies to report.

— Dr. Aarya Sen, Port Aurora Cell

The lie was clean.

The omission was careful.

And it was hers.

She hit **SAVE**.

A quiet click echoed in the hollow of the shelter. The tablet dimmed. The last bar of charge flickered—then steadied, as if waiting for its next command.

But Aarya had none to give.

She set it aside.

The child moved closer and rested her head lightly against Aarya's arm. The hum that followed was not the same as the ones before. It was softer, more intimate—an echo of breath, the space between heartbeat and silence.

And slowly, as if sensing it too, the woman looked up. Their eyes met.

No words. No nod. But in that look—a recognition.

Aarya was no longer just an outsider.

She was now something else.

Something in-between.

09:32 IST

The air had grown heavier.

Even the spores seemed to drift slower, their glow dimmer in the late morning haze. The forest held its breath. As if it, too, was waiting for something to be said.

The woman had gone silent, fingers still weaving strands of dried sporecaps. The child hummed no more. She sat beside Aarya, hands pressed to the soil, drawing the spiral deeper into the dirt with one steady finger.

Then he returned.

The male Gleamer, backlit by the thinned canopy, stepped into the clearing.

No sound. No ceremony. Just presence.

The child glanced up and stilled.

Aarya met his gaze—this time without flinching.

His eyes scanned the ground. The extinguished fire. The closed tablet.

Then, slowly, they rose to her.

He stepped forward—not aggressively, but deliberately.

The woman stood. Her body didn't tense, but shifted. Protective.

He spoke.

Short, guttural syllables that Aarya didn't understand, but felt. The tone was low, edged. A question. No—an accusation.

She didn't answer.

Not with words.

She reached for the child's hand again.

The male's eyes narrowed.

A pause.

Then he pointed—first to Aarya.

Then to the ridge beyond the trees.

Then to the sky.

His meaning was clear.

They're watching.

You brought them.

Aarya stood.

"*I know,*" she whispered.

He stepped closer.

Not threatening. But not trusting, either.

The child let go of Aarya's hand. Slipped back behind the woman. The air thinned.

The male's gaze did not waver.

He tapped his chest.

Then pointed to the soil.

Then to the trees.

Then again, to the ridge—where the shimmer of cloaked drones still lurked, just beyond sight.

Each gesture was clear:

We belong here.

They came from there.

You brought them back.

Aarya didn't argue. She couldn't.

Her presence had stirred the air.

And she didn't know if it could be unstirred.

But then—

He did something she hadn't expected.

He dropped to one knee.

And with one finger, he wiped away the spiral the child had drawn.

Erased it. Slowly. Cleanly.

Not in anger.

But in mourning.

Aarya froze.

The gesture struck her harder than any blow.

The child looked down. Not startled. Not afraid.

Just… understanding. As if she'd seen this before.

The woman said nothing.

And the hums—those low, warm strands of trust—remained absent.

Aarya felt it all shift.

The ache of being not unwelcome, but no longer welcome.

She reached down, hesitated—and then redrew the spiral. Her finger trembling.

One loop. Then another. Not perfect.

But present.

The male watched.

And then, with a short breath through his nose—he turned, stepped back into the trees, and vanished.

10:00 IST

The spiral still lay in the dirt—redrawn by her own hand.

But something about it felt… fragile now. Not sacred, not safe. As if the moment the male Gleamer erased it, it had ceased to belong.

Aarya stood. The fire had dimmed to embers. The hums had not returned.

Then came the tone.

Her tablet buzzed once, sharp and metallic. Not the soft pulse of system updates. This was direct—from Port Aurora, encrypted, blinking urgent.

She picked it up.

SURVEILLANCE PRIORITY ALERT — IICHA East Cell

Satellite echo confirmed: *Ridge Quadrant.*

Heat anomaly consistent with non-biological UAVs.

Unflagged entity class: *PLA scout drone.*

Altitude: 200m. Sweep pattern: Delta-Arc 3.

Upload pending logs for Sector E7 by 1600 IST.

— Auto-Auth: BioSynth Protocol Cell 4A

Aarya's hands stiffened around the device.

PLA.

She'd heard it in whispers at first. Then rumors. Then field jokes.

But now here it was—in writing, blinking from her own field terminal.

BioSynth wasn't just mapping the jungle.

They were sharing the map.

And then—memory cracked open like a seed.

Port Aurora Lab | 29 March 2075 | 17:34 IST

The storm outside had picked up. Leaves slapped against the metal louvers.

Inside, the lab was a glow of blue monitors and uneaten instant noodles.

Anjana was pacing.

"It's not just funding, Aarya. You know that, right? BioSynth isn't neutral. They're laundering research through legal shells—half their patents go to Hong Kong consortiums backed by the PLA."

Aarya sat frozen, tablet in hand.

"But IICHA is Indian. Our licenses—our ethics board—"

Meghana, from the corner:

"Our board is toothless. Half of them are careerists. Half of them are careerists. The other half don't even know where

South Veyra is. They rubber-stamp field work they'll never see."

Anjana stopped pacing.

"Page 48. Subsidiary clause. Read it."

Aarya scrolled.

There it was—buried under marine bioethics and fiscal disclosures: A string of foreign characters, embedded in legalese. Singaporean holding firm. Indirect minority stake. Cross-licensing of biome patents.

PLA owns 16.7% of BioSynth's offshore R&D pool.

Under NDA.

No obligation of host disclosure unless geopolitical risk is triggered.

The silence between them was longer than the storm outside.

"It's not research," Meghana had said, flatly.

"It's extraction."

"It's not research," Meghana had said, flatly.

"It's extraction."

That word rang loud as Aarya stared down at her tablet in the present, the drone alert still pulsing on-screen.

Extraction.

Not study.

Not stewardship.

Not science.

They weren't logging spore patterns for conservation.

They were mapping resource veins—and Gleamer blood, regenerative and radiant, was the richest deposit of all.

The drone wasn't looking for her anymore.

It was confirming what she had found.

She turned slowly. The clearing was empty now. The child and woman had withdrawn into the thicket of leaves and vine—as if they, too, had sensed something in the air shift.

Or maybe they just knew what came next.

The male Gleamer's warning came back in silence:

You brought them.

Aarya sank to her knees by the spiral in the dirt. The breeze had already begun to distort its shape—loops softened by dust, by time, by breath.

She touched it gently, as if it were a wound.

What happens to the spiral if I speak?

And what happens if I don't?

The forest beyond the grove rustled.

A sound like wings, or wind, or something in between.

She didn't look up.

She didn't need to.

The watchers were near.

Aarya closed the tablet.

It hissed faintly as it powered down, the screen folding into black like a sealed eye. The blinking drone alert silenced mid-flash, but its presence didn't leave. It hovered in the air now, invisible but felt—like pressure before a monsoon.

The spiral in the dirt had lost its form.

Winds had blurred the edges. What had once pulsed with meaning was now just lines in the earth—faint, scattered, half-erased.

She reached into her satchel and pulled out a small vial. One of her original sample tubes. Empty. Still clean.

She stared at it.

This is what they want.

Not soil. Not spores.

Blood. Healing. Patents.

She almost crushed it in her fist. But instead, she set it down—gently—beside the spiral's remains.

From the corner of the grove, the child returned. Her steps were silent. She said nothing.

She crouched by the line Aarya had redrawn earlier and touched it again.

A new spiral emerged—loop by loop—drawn between their fingers. Not perfect. But theirs.

And then, the hum returned.

Low. Soft. Almost inaudible at first. It slipped between the trees like mist, like memory.

This time, it came from all three—the woman's steady breath, the child's rising tone, and—somewhere farther back—even the male's resonance, buried but present.

Not in agreement. But in acknowledgment.

Aarya didn't speak.

She only hummed back.

And in that hum, for the first time, she felt not just forgiven.

She felt chosen.

The hum faded again—but not entirely. It lingered like warmth in coals, deep beneath the morning breeze.

Aarya pulled her bag closer and retrieved her field logbook—the paper one, bound in weathered green, with frayed ribbon markers and a spine soft from years of folding.

The IICHA-issued tablet sat next to it—powered down, sanctioned, encrypted.

This book was not.

She flipped past earlier pages—spore density charts, humidity logs, growth rings measured in hours and millimeters. Past the algorithm-synced entries.

And stopped on a blank page.

She picked up her pencil.

For a moment, her hand didn't move.

Then, slowly, she began to write:

"12 April 2075 — South Veyra Interior"

"Confirmed evidence of rapid cellular healing in child subject. Wound closed within seconds. No visible clotting or scarring. Blood: dark violet; viscosity low. Possible fungal symbiosis."

"Female subject's salve: complex. Herbal base with fungal oil infusion. Applied with rhythmic vibration and breath-hum, matching subject's pulse. Possible acoustic-biological feedback loop?"

She paused.

Looked at the trees.

At the child now curled beside the fire.

At the woman braiding vines, her eyes half-lidded but alert.

Then she wrote:

"They heal because they are in harmony."

"Not infected. Not altered. Whole."

"I will not give them to you."

She shut the notebook.

Not locked. Not encrypted.

But hers.

And somewhere far above, the drones swept in low arcs—recording everything but meaning.

11:52 IST

It began with a rustle.

Not the gentle stir of leaves overhead or the quiet steps of the child.

This was sharper. Low. Brief.

Then again—closer this time. A snap of undergrowth. A branch flexing beneath unexpected weight.

Aarya looked up from her notebook. The pencil paused mid-word.

The child tensed but didn't move. Her eyes shifted toward the tree line, gaze fixed.

The woman's hands stilled on the vine she was braiding. Her head tilted slightly—listening.

Even the fire cracked differently now.

The male Gleamer appeared at the edge of the clearing—not from the path he usually took, but from the far side, his shoulders squared, breath fast.

He made no sound, but the woman saw him and stood immediately.

Aarya rose too, the notebook clutched against her chest.

The male pointed.

Then raised his hand to his mouth and made a short, sharp sound.

Like a whistle.

But fractured.

Then again.

And a third time.

A signal.

The woman replied—not with a hum, but with a flat, rapid beat against her own chest. Once. Twice. Then silence.

The child stood now, slowly. The spiral forgotten in the dirt.

Aarya looked between them.

"What is it?" she whispered, instinctively.

No one answered.

But in the distance—faint, almost inaudible—a new hum rose from the forest.

Not theirs.

Not gentle.

It was mechanical. Angular.

Like something trying to imitate a hum but built from wire and script.

The hum deepened.

Not loud—but structured.

Synthetic.

Like something mimicking resonance without ever understanding it.

Aarya turned her ear toward the trees. The sound pulsed in short intervals—three notes, then silence. Three notes again.

Not a Gleamer hum.

A drone signature.

It wasn't hovering anymore.

It was searching.

The male Gleamer stepped toward Aarya, his jaw tight. His eyes moved fast—from the tree line, to the notebook in her hand, to the fire's ash. He pointed again—this time, not toward the ridge, but the base of a large, hollowed tree beyond the clearing.

Aarya hesitated.

The woman moved next—swift but calm—scooping the child up, cradling her close. Her hum was different now: lower, urgent, rhythmic.

A signal.

A shield.

The male gestured again—firmer now, toward the tree.

Aarya moved. Quickly.

She reached the trunk, crouched low, and slipped into the hollow. It wasn't deep, but wide enough to conceal her form in shadow. Dry leaves muffled the ground. The scent of fungus was stronger here—cleaner, even pleasant.

From within, she could still see them.

The male disappeared behind the edge of the grove.

The woman sat cross-legged before the fire, as if nothing had changed.

The child lay across her lap, eyes wide, breathing synced to the hum.

Then the sound came—closer.

A mechanical drone, gliding low, just beyond the clearing's edge. Not cloaked anymore.

Its hum buzzed—artificial and empty.

And still, the woman hummed back.

Not louder. Just steadier.

Not fear.

Not defiance.

But refusal.

Aarya crouched in the hollow, heart tight in her throat.

The drone's hum grew louder, more deliberate. She could hear the pulse of its rotors, fanned flat and low, sweeping the canopy as if it were peeling back the jungle leaf by leaf.

She held her breath.

Inside the tree, the air was damp and thick with fungal musk. The notebook trembled slightly in her grip.

Outside, the woman did not move.

She sat like a monument. A stone carved by the song of rain and memory. Her hum continued—low, exact, unwavering.

It wasn't a call.

It was a boundary.

The child's fingers wrapped in her mother's hair, eyes half-closed, calm. A small vibration escaped her throat. It met her mother's tone like a thread tying two branches.

Together, the sound was not quite human.

Not quite anything else either.

Then—

A change in pitch.

The drone stalled above the clearing.

Aarya's stomach turned.

It hovered.

Buzzed once.

Then again.

A small flash of red blinked from its undercarriage.

It's scanning.

Still the hum continued.

Not louder. Not panicked.

But exact.

Like a shield being held up in silence.

Aarya's fingers clenched around the notebook. Not because of fear. But because she understood:

They weren't hiding her with noise.

They were shielding her with song.

And in that moment, for the first time since arriving on South Veyra, Aarya didn't feel like she was studying something wild.

She felt like she was being kept alive by something ancient.

And chosen.

The drone hovered.

For a moment, it didn't move—suspended like a thought between decision and dismissal.

Aarya stayed still, crouched inside the hollow tree, one hand pressed against bark, the other wrapped around her notebook. She could hear the engine's soft churn—so faint it barely disturbed the leaves.

The woman's hum continued.

It didn't rise or shift.

It simply held.

The child matched it now, her breath threading perfectly with her mother's tone. The melody—if it could even be called that—was simple, circular, patient.

A harmony not made to deter, but to belong.

The drone clicked.

A single red blink on its underside.

Scanning complete.

Then—

It rose.

One slow meter at a time, its sound ascending with it. No shift in pattern. No descent. No alarm.

It drifted upward through the trees, disappeared past the canopy, and was gone.

Aarya exhaled.

The grove remained still for several long seconds after the drone vanished—as if the forest itself was making sure it had really left.

Then the woman released her breath. The child uncurled.

And from the trees, the male returned—his eyes scanning the clearing.

He said nothing.

But he looked at Aarya.

Directly.

She stepped out of the hollow. Slowly. Not in apology, but in understanding.

No one spoke.

The fire cracked once. A single pop.

The hums faded into quiet.

But in that silence—there was no fear.

There was only presence.

And something else.

Permission.

She didn't realize how cold she'd been until she stepped from the hollow.

The air wrapped around her shoulders like wet silk. But the fire's warmth—gentle, low, steady—reached her skin and settled deeper than heat. It didn't chase the chill. It welcomed her back.

The fire cracked again—softer this time. Not urgent. Just alive.

She lowered herself beside it, careful not to intrude. The woman didn't look at her, but neither did she turn away. The child leaned into her lap again, her eyes flicking once toward Aarya, then down to the spiral that had almost been erased.

The wind passed through the grove like a breath released after holding too long.

Aarya opened her notebook again—but she didn't write.

Not yet.

Instead, she looked at the page she had last written—the one where she had logged the healing, the hums, and the choice to remain silent.

She traced the words with her thumb.

"They heal because they are in harmony."

"Not infected. Not altered. Whole."

Then she added, almost absently, as if the words had waited inside her:

"They are not data points."

"They are memory."

She shut the book again.

The woman began to hum—not the defensive tone from before, but something quieter. Lower. The kind of sound that might come from stirring soup, or winding a child's braid, or watching light shift across the floor.

Aarya listened.

It was not a song.

It was a space being held.

And she didn't feel hidden anymore.

She felt held.

Then—just as she let her shoulders drop, breath deepen, something shifted in the corner of her awareness.

She glanced toward the deeper edge of the grove, where the trees thickened into shadow. The light didn't quite reach there. But still—something watched.

Not a figure. Not a shape.

Just a presence. Felt, not seen.

As if there were others beyond the clearing—waiting, or withdrawing, or simply measuring her silence.

Not hostile.

But listening.

Aarya stood again—not quickly, not out of need. Just curiosity.

She stepped past the fire, past the low mat of woven reeds, past the still-burning salve bowl. The woman didn't stop her. The child didn't stir.

The grove narrowed into a thicket of fig and fern, the kind that caught wind in their roots and whispered nothing back. She moved slowly, pressing each footfall into soft leaf mulch.

The silence here was different.

Not empty—held.

Like stepping into a memory that wasn't hers.

And then she saw it.

A second firepit. Cold now, its ash scattered but shaped. Stones in a wide ring, the interior swept clean. Nearby: a woven sleeping mat, rolled but recently used. A wooden ladle—carved with spiral motifs—lay on its side, damp from last night's rain.

And on a moss-covered stump, an object she hadn't seen before:

A mask.

Made from bark, hollowed and smoothed, painted with streaks of ochre and green. It had no eyes—only a spiral carved at the forehead, as if the vision was meant to face inward.

She reached toward it—then stopped.

Not because she was afraid.

Because she understood:

This wasn't forgotten.

This was left behind on purpose.

And someone would know she'd seen it.

She stepped back.

Somewhere deeper in the trees, a branch shifted.

No voice called out.

But something old—something waiting—turned its gaze.

The mask stayed with her.

Not its weight—she hadn't touched it—but its silence. That silence felt full, like a sealed jar of water. It followed her as she stepped carefully back toward the clearing.

She didn't rush.

Didn't look over her shoulder.

But she felt it.

The understanding—not quite permission, not quite warning. Just a pulse of presence. The kind that exists when something ancient decides to observe you and nothing else.

Back at the fire, the woman was still seated.

She glanced up as Aarya approached, not startled, not stern. She said nothing. But her eyes lingered, long enough to say:

You saw something.

Aarya didn't speak.

She only nodded. A small thing.

Not confession. Just acknowledgment.

The child looked up too, as if she could smell the difference in Aarya's breath. She leaned slightly, as if about to speak, then stopped—and simply placed a hand on Aarya's forearm as she sat beside her.

Not a question.

Just contact.

Aarya let it rest there.

The fire crackled again.

And the male emerged—this time not from the far trees, but from the clearing's northern edge, near the sleeping mats. He paused when he saw Aarya back at the fire, his gaze sharp. Then it softened—just slightly.

He didn't approach.

But he didn't vanish either.

Instead, he stood at the boundary where shadow met sun, watching.

A sentinel.

A reminder.

A memory with muscle.

Aarya looked at all of them—then back at her hands.

There was dirt beneath her nails, ash on her sleeves, and something humming faintly in her chest—not song, not sickness, but a rhythm that wasn't hers and somehow fit.

She didn't write.

She didn't speak.

She simply remained.

And for the first time since stepping onto South Veyra, she didn't feel like she was waiting to leave.

She felt like she was waiting to be asked to stay.

The clearing had returned to rhythm.

The woman resumed weaving. The child began to trace patterns in the ash with her fingertip. Even the fire, trimmed low and careful, moved with the confidence of a place that had nothing left to defend—only to endure.

Aarya sat near them, legs drawn in, elbows on her knees, her back aching from tension that had only just begun to release.

Her tablet remained untouched.

The notebook remained closed.

And yet—she felt more recorded than ever.

Because they had seen her now.

Not the IICHA.

Not BioSynth.

Them.

The watchers beneath the canopy. The ones behind the mask.

How long had they been listening?

Long before I heard them, they heard me.

She turned her head slowly, eyes brushing the edge of the grove where the second firepit had stood, where the mask had waited like a riddle left out in the rain.

She could still feel its weight—not heavy, but rooted.

And with it, a thought unspoken:

What if I've been looking through the wrong lens?

Not as a scientist.

But as a stranger.

Not all truths want to be mapped.

Some just want to be remembered.

She looked down at her palms.

Soil. Ash. A scratch that hadn't quite healed.

Marks of care, not violence.

The child shifted closer.

And without thinking, Aarya placed her hand over the child's—just for a moment.

Not to study.

Not to confirm.

But to stay.

A breeze stirred the canopy.

The leaves shifted in a rhythm that mimicked breath—deep, slow, measured. The fire had settled into a bed of embers, soft as coals under moonlight. The grove was calm again.

But calm was not the same as safe.

Aarya lifted her gaze toward the canopy. There were no drones now. No shimmer in the light. But she had learned something today.

Silence does not mean they've stopped watching.

She reached for her tablet once more—not to activate it, but to tuck it back into her satchel. Covered. Closed.

Her notebook remained in her lap, the last page marked with spirals and partial thoughts. She had not written the word "Gleamer" once.

She didn't need to.

They were not a category.

They were a choice.

The woman stood and gathered herbs. The child curled beside the ash pit, humming faintly—a thread of sound that wasn't for comfort or signal now.

It was just... living.

From the edge of the trees, the male Gleamer watched. His arms crossed. Not harshly. Just firmly. A presence reminding her: she had not been forgiven.

She had simply not been removed.

Aarya stood and dusted her hands. She looked toward the trees. And beyond them.

Back in Port Aurora, her comms would be blinking.

Her name would be searched.

And somewhere, a server—funded by BioSynth, coded in partnership with a foreign state—would register that no anomaly reports had been filed from South Veyra.

She hadn't lied.

She had simply chosen not to betray them.

The wind carried the hum across her skin like a warning wrapped in warmth.

And she knew:

They had kept her.

But they had not claimed her.

That part—still—would be hers to decide.

***

Chapter 5: The Claim

The sketch came before the sound.

Thin lines curved across parchment—spiraling, expanding, not drawn by hand but blooming, like something alive beneath the page. Aarya saw the spore-form emerge slowly, exact and soft, the graphite catching where her father's pencil hesitated at a curve. A blur of his voice hummed behind her. No words. Just breath, deep and calm. The morning sun outside the Shyambazar flat leaked golden through the shutters.

"They live," he murmured. Not to her. To the page.

She was nine again, watching from the edge of his study mat, hugging her knees, afraid to blink in case the spore vanished. The mug of tea beside him steamed gently, untouched. A radio low in the background. Something old—Kaushiki Chakraborty—woven into the morning like incense.

Then the line broke.

The sketch stuttered. The graphite snapped.

Her father looked up.

His eyes were soft. Tired. Filled with the kind of knowing she wouldn't understand until years later. His smile didn't hold joy, but something stranger—something like sorrow wrapped in awe.

"They remember, Aaru. Even when we don't."

A flicker of something—heat, light—ran across the spiral he'd drawn. It shimmered. A thread of mycelium lifting from the page.

She reached out—

And woke.

The grove was quiet.

The hum hadn't begun yet. The fire was unlit. Morning held its breath in mist. But the image of the spiral still floated behind her eyes—drawn not by a scientist, not by a child, but by something that lived beneath both.

She pressed her palm to the dirt beside her mat.

It was warm.

And waiting.

The child appeared first.

Barefoot, her steps barely pressed into the damp soil, she emerged from the mist like she had always been part of it. No words. Just a nod—a gesture that wasn't a command but an offering.

She held out something small and wrapped in a leaf.

Aarya took it gently. The wrapping unfurled to reveal a paste—thick, amber-green, smelling of ash and something fermented. She recognized the scent faintly from the day they had healed her.

The child pointed toward the outer ring of the grove. A flat stone rested there, shallow grooves etched into its surface. Bowls of dried herbs and fungus had been arranged nearby, orderly but rough. It looked like a workbench, or something older.

A ritual table.

Aarya moved, careful not to misstep. Her fingers tingled slightly from the paste's residue—its warmth spreading into her knuckles.

The woman was already there.

She didn't speak, didn't even meet Aarya's eyes—just nodded once, then showed her the motion: grind, mix, hum.

A rhythm, not just of hands—but of breath. A cyclical motion that felt less like preparation and more like listening.

Aarya mimicked it—awkwardly at first. Her paste scattered, and the hum in her throat cracked, uncertain.

The woman corrected her without touch. Just a glance. A reshaped breath.

And Aarya tried again.

Slower this time.

A few beats passed.

Then the child joined the hum.

Soft. Threaded.

Like a third voice in a song that was never written, only passed down through muscle and dust.

Aarya's shoulders dropped.

The paste in her palm thickened—reacting slightly, the surface pulsing once like a heartbeat.

The woman stopped. Looked at her.

Then, for the first time, reached out—not to guide, but to place her own palm gently over Aarya's.

Their fingers didn't press.

They simply met.

And Aarya understood:

This wasn't teaching.

This was welcoming.

The woman lifted her hand.

Aarya's remained, palm open, a thin smear of paste glowing faintly in the light. Not bright. Not unnatural. Just… responsive. Like morning dew shifting with breath.

Then it happened.

A small, quiet rhythm beneath her skin. Not her heartbeat.

Softer. Slower. External.

It thrummed once—like a memory of touch.

Then again.

Aarya's eyes didn't widen, but her breath caught.

The pulse was gentle, almost imagined.

But it was there.

Her fingers flexed slightly, not out of control, but in instinct.

The child, watching from a crouch nearby, smiled—not giddy, not surprised. As though she'd seen it before. As though she expected it.

Aarya looked at her hands.

Not trembling.

But tuned.

As if the skin had become aware of what lay beneath it—not muscle or bone, but something older. Something shared.

The paste began to dry along her palm, but the pulse lingered. Slower now. Just two beats more.

Then quiet.

The woman rose and moved toward a line of stacked bark trays, placing her bowl down with quiet certainty.

The ritual was complete.

But Aarya stayed seated, hand still open, the spiral's ghost in her fingers, and that echo of rhythm nestled just under the surface.

Not infection.

Not hallucination.

A reply.

For the first time, she didn't wonder what it meant.

She only wondered if they felt it too.

07:02 IST

The tablet buzzed.

No tone. Just a silent tremor against the satchel where she'd buried it days ago. The sound didn't belong in the grove. Not among hums and wind. But it found her anyway.

Aarya wiped her hand on her thigh and unlatched the flap.

The screen flickered once—faint in the morning light—and then bloomed open.

IICHA | Port Aurora Satellite Node

TO: Field Biologist SEN, A. [SE-ID: IICHA.2075.04.09]

SUBJECT: Report Deviation | Section E7 | BioSynth Shared Tag

"Confirmation Pending. No observable transmission logged from Sector E7 in 48.0 hr cycle.

BioSynth has initiated preliminary risk assessment.

Field Operator flagged for sample extraction delay.

Response window ends 13.04.75 | 20:00 IST.

Kindly upload E7 data. If compromised, initiate CODE: SOLACE."

—Auto-Auth: Dr. D. Dey (Field Surveillance Cell)

Her thumb hovered above the screen.

"CODE: SOLACE."

She'd heard of it once, whispered in a lab corridor in Port Aurora. A euphemism for extraction, but not the peaceful kind. If triggered, a drone wouldn't ask for a response. It would collect what it needed.

Even if what it needed was blood.

She stared at the blinking cursor.

Baba had once told her, "Sometimes silence is louder than any cry. But some silences—they become permissions."

Was this one of them?

She shut the screen.

The grove was still. The hums hadn't resumed. The woman watched her from across the fire, not moving, but alert. The child sat beside her, drawing something invisible into the dirt with her fingertip.

They didn't ask what the message said.

They didn't have to.

The forest already knew.

Port Aurora Field Lab | 29 March 2075 | 17:48 IST

The light inside the Port Aurora lab had a way of turning blue by evening—washed in screen-glow and condensation. Outside, the rain drummed the roof in steady rhythm. Inside, Anjana leaned against the lab counter, arms folded, gaze fixed on Aarya's assignment tablet.

"You sure about this, Aars?"

Aarya hadn't looked up. She was syncing terrain maps and standard fungal profiles—South Veyra, Sector E7. Remote. Dense. Underflagged.

"It's just mapping. Same as always."

Anjana exhaled through her teeth.

"They don't send us solo anymore. Not unless the site's too hot for teams. Or too quiet to come back from."

Aarya turned. *"It was approved. Dr. Dey signed off."*

Anjana shook her head, half-smile bitter.

"Dey signs off on what BioSynth greenlights. And BioSynth loves solo ops—less overhead, less liability."

"Less witnesses," Meghana murmured from across the lab, not looking up from her sequencing.

Aarya paused.

"You think it's a setup?"

Meghana shrugged. *"Not a setup. A sieve. See what comes back. If anything."*

Anjana moved closer, voice low now, conspiratorial.

"You remember CODE: SOLACE?"

"Whispers."

"It's not a myth. It's a protocol. Silent extraction. If your feed drops for 72 hours, they send something in. Not a chopper. A drone. No questions. No trace."

Aarya held her breath.

The rain intensified.

Anjana touched the screen, scrolling past a clause buried in the contract:

"Field recovery waived if risk deemed external or political."

"Solo missions aren't about trust," she said.

"They're about silence."

South Veyra Island | 13 April 2075 | 07:15 IST

Aarya blinked.

The fire cracked. The woman was still watching her.

She reached for her notebook, not the tablet. Opened to a blank page.

But she didn't write yet.

She just stared at the spiral in her mind. The one Baba had drawn. The one the spores now pulsed with.

And she whispered to herself:

"They sent me alone… so I couldn't bring anything back."

The notebook lay open on her lap.

The blank page waited.

The pencil hovered.

But Aarya couldn't move yet. Her hand felt too heavy—not with fear, but with the weight of knowing.

The child shifted closer.

Small fingers, dust-streaked and sure, dipped into the loose ash near the fire's edge. No hesitation. No glance toward Aarya.

Slowly, patiently, the child began to draw.

Not a figure.

Not letters.

A spiral.

One line. Then another. Coiling outward, wider with each loop, but never hurried.

The pattern flowed from wrist to fingertip with the same care Aarya had once seen in her father—quiet reverence, not control.

Aarya leaned forward without thinking.

Her breath caught.

It wasn't exact—but close enough that the hairs on her arms lifted.

The same structure.

The same slow expansion.

The living memory of a shape that didn't belong to maps or microscopes—but to something deeper.

Something remembered.

The child finished the spiral and lifted her finger. A smudge of ash clung to her fingertip. She pressed it gently against Aarya's forearm, just above the wrist—a single mark, a soft black print, fading as fast as it was made.

Aarya didn't flinch.

She looked at the spiral.

Then at the child.

The woman across the fire gave the smallest of nods—not permission, not command.

Just acknowledgment.

You see it now.

The pulse under Aarya's skin flickered once.

And she understood.

Not in language.

Not in science.

In memory.

They weren't giving her the spiral.

They were showing her that she already carried it.

The ash spiral blurred as the morning wind stirred.

Aarya shielded it with one hand, cradling the fragile lines while she reached with the other for her notebook.

She turned the page—past blank spaces meant for mapped decay, past half-formed observations about humidity and spore density.

Past everything she had come here to write.

Fresh paper. A soft page, still smelling of starch and promise.

She pressed her pencil against it.

For a moment, her hand hovered.

Then she drew.

Not a perfect spiral—her fingers still stiff, the graphite catching on fibers—but she sketched the line the child had traced. Around and outward. Breathing between each curl.

She wrote no measurements.

No tags.

No coordinates.

Only a single line at the top of the page:

"Memory Sketch | 13.04.2075 | South Veyra | Uncatalogued."

She underlined "Uncatalogued" twice, lightly.

It wasn't rebellion.

It was return.

The notebook closed with a soft sound.

Not hidden.

Not encrypted.

Simply closed.

The woman stood and scattered fresh herbs into the fire, their scent blooming in a thick, green wave.

The child smeared a new mark into the ash, already forgetting the last one, already making the next.

And somewhere far beyond the trees, beyond the thin song of the drone wings still searching, still circling, Aarya felt a tether snap loose.

Not the one tying her to the Grove.

The one tying her to Port Aurora.

08:04 IST

The fire burned low, fragrant with the oils of crushed leaves.

The spiral was tucked safely between the pages of her notebook, the ash mark faded from her skin but not from memory.

Aarya stretched her legs, feeling the dampness cling to her clothes, the cool seep into her boots.

She might have stayed there—might have let herself sink fully into the hush of the grove, where breath and soil and hums braided together in a rhythm older than any law she'd ever signed—

But then she heard it.

Not the drone.

Not the forest's whisper.

A crack.

Farther upslope. Beyond the ridge line that separated the Gleamers' sanctuary from the wider jungle.

Not a branch breaking under weight—no animal.

126

A boot.

A human step.

The woman heard it too.

Her head lifted—not alarmed, but alert, her shoulders tilting subtly toward the child.

The male appeared from the other side of the clearing, fast but quiet. He signed something with his hands—sharp, clipped motions. A warning.

Aarya rose slowly, her satchel already slung.

Her skin tingled again—but this time, it wasn't the spores.

It was instinct.

The tablet in her bag vibrated once, briefly, a single silent pulse—an incoming signal, low-frequency, meant for field tracking.

They were looking for her.

They were closer than she thought.

The child looked up at her—eyes steady, not pleading, not fearful.

Just present.

You chose to stay, the look said.

Now choose what to protect.

The hums didn't rise this time.

The forest waited.

And so did she.

Another crack echoed, sharper this time.

Closer.

Aarya pressed herself lower against the embankment that rimmed the grove's far side, the undergrowth clutching at her sleeves. She felt the woman's gaze across the clearing, steady but unreadable. The male had disappeared into the trees already, a shadow among shadows.

The child remained by the fire.

Still.

Waiting.

Another vibration from her satchel.

Short. Urgent.

She slipped the tablet halfway from the pack just enough to glance at the screen.

A new directive blinked in muted red:

"Field Status: Extraction Proximity 2 km. Initiate Rendezvous Point Alpha."

She closed her eyes.

They weren't just scanning now.

They were advancing.

A clearing. A recovery drone. Maybe even armed retrievers if she didn't comply fast enough.

For a brief second, she thought about it.

Walking out.

Presenting herself.

Saying the right things.

"Field sample inconclusive."

"Environmental interference."

"Subject not located."

Keeping the spiral, the pulse, the hums safe inside her, where no drone could catalog them.

And herself?

Filed away.

As "recovered."

As "uncontaminated."

As "data."

But then the child looked at her again.

Not asking for help.

Not begging.

Just believing she wouldn't betray what had been shared.

Aarya's stomach turned—not in fear, but in something heavier.

Grief.

Not for herself.

But for what would be lost if she let the silence be broken by the wrong voice.

She closed the tablet.

Sealed it back into the satchel.

And without a word, she moved back toward the center of the grove—closer to the fire, closer to the spiral etched still faintly in ash.

The woman watched her.

And this time, gave a slow, almost imperceptible nod.

Stay.

But choose to stay.

The wind shifted.

Somewhere beyond the ridge, metal cracked against rock—equipment being hauled, orders barked low over encrypted bands.

But inside the grove, there was only the soft scrape of ash under Aarya's boots. The fire's smoke climbed thin and slow into the morning mist.

She knelt.

The notebook was heavy in her hands—not from weight, but from everything it now carried. Not just data. Not just observation.

Memory.

She touched the spiral the child had drawn. The lines still lingered in the ash, faint but stubborn, curling outward like a secret that refused to die.

And suddenly—without warning—the old memory broke through.

Not the dream.

Not Baba's calm sketches.

But that day.

Shyambazar | Kolkata | 18 July 2070 | Late Afternoon

The storm had lashed the shutters. The river had breached its banks again. She was seventeen, pacing the cracked floorboards, soaked from running home across flooded lanes.

Inside, smoke.

Baba's papers—his mycelium sketches, his diagrams of fungal dreams—fed a small fire in the kitchen basin.

Ma stood over it, jaw tight, fists white.

Aarya screamed.

"What are you doing? What are you doing?!"

Ma didn't look at her. Just shoved another handful into the flame.

The smoke smelled sharp—paper and ink and loss.

When Ma finally spoke, her voice broke like splintered glass:

"I lost your father to them.

I won't lose you too."

Aarya grabbed at the burning pages, but Ma slapped her hand away.

The sketch she managed to save—half-scorched, half-erased—crumpled in her fists, blackening her palms.

She ran from the kitchen, from the house, from the city if she could have.

She never forgave Ma for that.

Not really.

Not even now.

South Veyra Island | 13 April 2075 | 08:26 IST

Aarya pressed her hand into the ash, leaving a print beside the spiral.

A second spiral—cruder, messier—but touching the first.

A bridge.

Not erasing.

Not burning.

Adding.

She wiped her eyes with the back of her wrist, smearing ash along her cheekbone.

The woman by the fire saw. Said nothing.

The child hummed a single note—low, warm, vibrating into the bones of the earth.

And Aarya understood.

Ma had tried to protect her by destroying what Baba left behind.

But this forest protected differently.

It remembered.

It sheltered scars and songs and sketches alike.

And now it sheltered her.

Not because she was untouched.

Because she was marked.

Because she chose to be.

The drone's hum rose faintly beyond the treeline.

No orders barked yet.

No extraction initiated.

But it was close enough that she could smell the metallic static leaking into the air.

Aarya stood.

No panic. No rush.

She tucked the notebook against her chest, wrapping both arms around it—not like a scientist carrying a field log.

Like a daughter carrying something fragile from a burning house.

The child stepped to her side, pressing her small hand into Aarya's thigh, steadying her.

The woman nodded once.

The male Gleamer, silent in the trees, vanished into mist.

Aarya turned her back to the ridge.

Turned her face to the fire.

The extraction signal pulsed once more in her satchel—ignored.

She closed her eyes.

And chose.

***

Interlude: Pt. Aurora - Internal Memorandum

IICHA Field HQ. Port Aurora | 13 April 2075 | 08:52 IST

INTERNAL MEMORANDUM

Confidential: Field Surveillance Cell

Subject: Operational Review — Field Biologist SEN, A. (SE-ID: IICHA.2075.04.09)

Prepared by: Dr. Devdan Dey (Regional Coordinator, IICHA Port Aurora)

Executive Summary:

Field Operative SEN, Aarya, assigned South Veyra Island (Sector E7) April 9, 2075, under BioSynth-Fungal Decay Survey Initiative exceeded the standard reporting lapse window. No acceptable samples uploaded, transmission gaps found over the last 48.0 hrs.

Preliminary escalation requested by BioSynth representatives indicated by "irreplaceable field time sensitivity." CODE: SOLACE parameters were reviewed but deferred pending final notice.

Field Risk Assessment:

Terrain: Veteran high-risk/high-containment site (not mapped publicly past 2060 incident).

Operative Medical Status: Suggested pre-mission spore infection probability noted (Case Report 09/2075). Recall authorization was not activated.

Operative Psychological Profile: Mild noncompliance exhibited at previous postings (i.e., refusal to alter sample yields in accordance with commercialization yield metrics), otherwise low risk of political agitation.

Current Concerns:

An extended period of silence increases chances of external recovery exposure (in this case, PLA drone sweeps, logged 2 km offshore on 12 April 2075).

Possible contamination event: High Likelihood (Gleamer interaction risk > 48%, based on pre-mission terrain data projections).

Data loss risk rated as Critical.

Strategic Recommendations:

Let passive observance happen until 14 April 2075 0600 IST.

If it continues to be quiet, initiate SOLACE recovery protocol without further field notification.

In order to avoid later inquiries, omit internal records of operatives dispatched as singletons under classified tags.

Internal Note (Not for Circulation):

SEN, Aarya was an ideal candidate: passionate, solitary, and reached an instinctual thinking through personal legacy (ref. deceased parental figure SEN, Arun).

I regret her silence.

I live in hope for her recovery.

We need to let ourselves focus on the viability of the project.

Dr. Devdan Dey

Field Surveillance Coordinator, IICHA Port Aurora

***

Chapter 6: The Memory Grove

The light was different that morning.

It wasn't the mist, though it curled around the low ferns like breath. It wasn't the fire, though the embers still whispered in the pit. It wasn't even the absence of hums, which had become as steady as her own heartbeat.

There was something softer.

A settling.

A gathering.

An earnest slowness that moved through the grove, invisible, but thick as sap rising.

The woman knelt at the edge of the clearing, weaving thin strips of bark into low, tight braids. Her hands placed the strips around each other with regularity, slowly, without rush or need for ceremony.

The child crouched nearby, pulling leaves from a low branch, one at a time—breaking the leaves away and sorting them into piles by shade and shape.

Even the male Gleamer, who had never lingered long before, stood among the shadows at the grove's edge—not intervening, not patrolling—simply present.

Aarya sat cross-legged near the cooling fire, notebook unopened on her lap, feeling it all without fully understanding.

Not a ritual.

Not a warning.

An invitation.

She could taste it in the air—bitter and sweet, like fruit left too long in the sun.

She watched as the woman bundled the bark braids into a coil, binding them with vines. The woman's hum was so low Aarya could barely hear it, more a vibration through the ground than a sound in the air.

No one spoke.

No one gestured.

But somehow, Aarya knew.

Today was not for recording.

Not for hunting data.

Today was for following.

She placed her notebook gently beside the firepit—an offering of sorts—and rose to her feet.

The child smiled, bare toes digging into the soil, then darted lightly toward a thin seam in the ferns where the trees grew thicker, darker.

The woman followed.

Without a word, Aarya stepped after them—into a part of the forest that seemed to draw breath as she approached.

The mist swallowed them whole.

And the grove behind her disappeared.

The air thickened the farther they walked.

It wasn't suffocating—no heat pressing against her lungs—but a density she could feel in her skin, as if the atmosphere itself had deepened, grown more deliberate.

Each step sank slightly into moss so lush it swallowed sound.

The trees towered, older than she could comprehend, their roots coiling like sleeping serpents across the ground. Fungal webs climbed their trunks—glowing faintly even in daylight, a greenish blush under the bark.

The light here wasn't clear.

It fractured through mist and mycelium threads, breaking into soft spectrums—blues, greens, pale violets—that drifted across her field of vision like breath across glass.

The woman moved without hesitation, ducking under a low-hanging branch, her hands brushing spores into the air with a casual grace.

The child skipped ahead, toes flickering like fish in shallow water, arms outstretched to part the ferns as if she were swimming.

Aarya followed.

No hesitation.

Her body adjusted without thinking—slowing her pace, softening her footsteps, matching the invisible rhythm of the place.

She noticed, somewhere distantly, that her breath had synchronized with the movement of the mist.

In—when it thickened.

Out—when it thinned.

The pulse beneath her skin—the faint spore-borne heartbeat she had first felt days ago—thrummed again, not loudly, but steadily, like a key turning slowly in a long-forgotten lock.

She touched the bark spiral tucked into her satchel, hidden close to her ribs.

Not protection.

A reminder.

She belonged to something now—not because she had conquered it, not because she had mapped it, but because she had listened.

Ahead, the woman and child veered left, down a sloping trail that seemed to vanish into a grove so dense it might have been a memory rather than a place.

Aarya hesitated only once—just a breath—

Then followed them into the dark.

The slope leveled.

The mist thinned—not vanishing, but lifting, parting in delicate threads to reveal the space beyond.

Aarya stopped, breath catching quietly in her chest.

The trees widened into a natural cathedral—arches of intertwined roots and branches, thick with luminous fungi.

Webs of mycelium laced the canopy above, glimmering in patterns too intricate for her mind to map.

The air tasted different here.

Sweet, but sharp.

Alive.

Every inhalation felt like pulling old light into her lungs.

In the center of the clearing, a low basin carved into stone pulsed with faint light—like the memory of a heartbeat.

Around it, woven into the earth, were other shapes.

Not plants.

Not animals.

Figures.

She blinked.

At first she thought the mist played tricks—but no.

They were there.

Others.

Shapes that moved without sound between the columns of fungal bark and hanging vines.

Silhouettes brushing spores into the air with the barest touch of their hands.

Bare feet stirring the moss.

Some crouched by the stone basin, tending to the glowing threads that rose like steam.

Some knelt, palms pressed into the soil, as if listening through their skin.

None of them looked at her directly.

But she knew they saw her.

The child at her side simply stood still, allowing her to see, to understand.

Aarya's pulse slowed.

Not fear.

Not awe.

Something quieter.

The ache of realizing you had always been the intruder, even when you thought yourself alone.

The woman moved ahead, her braid swinging lightly against her spine, walking toward the basin with the same reverence Aarya remembered from temple courtyards back in Kolkata—the way her Baba had once walked around the giant banyan at Dakshineswar, muttering a prayer half under his breath, half into the roots.

They remember.

Not history, Aarya realized.

Living memory.

Woven into soil and body.

Kept alive by those who refused to forget.

She stepped forward, heart steady.

The mist curled around her ankles like welcome.

And the Grove, without word or gesture, accepted her into its breathing memory.

06:24 IST

The woman approached the basin first.

She knelt, palms brushing the moss at its rim, bowing her head briefly—not in submission, but in acknowledgment, as if greeting something older than language.

The child mirrored her, small knees folding easily into the damp earth.

Aarya hesitated at the edge, feeling the pull in her chest, low and certain.

The basin wasn't filled with water.

It held mist—thick and silver, coiling in slow, deliberate spirals that rose and fell in unseen rhythms.

Fine threads of fungal filaments floated in the vapor, catching the bioluminescent glow, each strand bending minutely to unseen pulses.

The surface wasn't still.

It breathed.

And with every breath, memory rose.

Not images.

Not words.

Feelings.

A tide of warmth. A shiver of grief. The sharp tang of fear.

The thick, honeyed ache of love too vast for skin to hold.

Aarya lowered herself slowly, knees brushing the moss, fingers splaying into the rich, damp soil.

The mist curled upward, brushing her forearms, her throat, the hollow behind her ears.

Not invasive.

Not demanding.

Just...asking.

She closed her eyes.

Inhaled.

The mist slid into her nostrils, her lungs—not choking, not burning.

Cool and dense, like breathing through a dream.

The pulse she'd first felt back in the grove—faint, tentative—returned now, stronger.

But it wasn't hers.

It was the grove's.

Her blood answered it.

She felt it: the spiral patterns tightening and loosening along her bones, threads that weren't visible, but which tied her breath, her body, into the breathing earth beneath her.

The mist thickened.

Her knees sank slightly deeper.

The woman beside her hummed—not a song, but a vibration, tuning the space.

The child leaned closer, pressing her small palm against Aarya's upper arm.

The figures beyond the mist watched, still silent.

Aarya opened her palms to the basin, letting the mist bathe her skin.

This was not data to log.

This was not an artifact to preserve.

This was an inheritance to carry.

The basin pulsed once more—low and wide—and something inside her pulsed back.

Not in submission.

In belonging.

The mist shifted.

It thickened around Aarya's wrists, ankles, collarbone—spooling, tethering—until she could no longer tell where her skin ended and the Grove began.

The hums deepened.

Not from any single throat, but from the ground itself.

She closed her eyes.

The first memory struck like a soft wave:

Not vision—sensation.

The press of muddy feet sprinting across wet jungle floor.

A sharp stone cutting the arch of a child's foot.

The rasp of hot breath.

The metallic clang of a foreign voice shouting behind trees.

Fear.

Raw. Animal.

Not hers.

Not now.

But real.

She gasped, clutching her knees.

The mist thickened again.

The second memory followed—cooler, slower:

A hand—brown, rough, steady—skimming along a fungal wall, humming softly, charting the patterns.

A sense of wonder folded into ache.

The knowledge of death nearby, but life blooming louder anyway.

Not knowledge she had read.

Knowledge, she felt.

The mist turned violet at the edges, spores pulsing in time with her breath.

Third memory:

Fire.

Smoke choking the Grove.

Not burning trees—burning spores, living archives.

Figures scattering spores into the air like prayers, desperate to save what could not be rewritten.

Loss.

But not surrender.

The hum rose inside her—unbidden—her vocal cords vibrating without her will, matching the low tone of the woman, the child, the unseen figures kneeling beyond.

She wasn't dreaming.

She wasn't hallucinating.

She was remembering with them.

Through them.

The mist coiled tight, one final shudder.

Aarya pressed both hands into the moss, forehead bowing without thought.

Tears slid unnoticed down her cheeks—not from sadness, not from fear, but from recognition.

She wasn't just breathing spores.

She was breathing ancestry.

Not her own lineage by blood.

Her lineage by belonging.

The Grove's memory wrapped itself around her heart and did not let go.

The mist loosened its grip.

It didn't vanish.

It simply thinned, like a breath slowly exhaled.

Shapes emerged again: trees, roots, the weaving patterns of fungus trailing like constellations across the soil.

The child sat cross-legged beside the basin now, humming softly to herself, tracing invisible patterns into the moss with one finger.

The woman knelt opposite Aarya, a small object cupped between her palms.

She extended it forward—not thrusting it, not offering it like a tool—but unfolding her hands with the same slow reverence she had shown the basin itself.

Aarya leaned closer.

It was a coil of spore-thread, barely the size of her thumbnail, woven with a delicate braid of bark and dried moss.

Simple.

But unmistakably deliberate.

A symbol.

A seed.

A mark.

The woman didn't gesture what to do with it.

She didn't need to.

Aarya reached out, hands trembling slightly—not from fear, but from the unbearable gentleness of it—and accepted the coil into her palm.

The threads were warm.

Alive.

Pulsing faintly, almost undetectably, against her skin.

Not as a command.

Not as a claim.

As recognition.

Aarya lifted it carefully to the hollow of her throat and pressed it there—where the hum she'd found in the Grove vibrated most steadily in her body.

The woman's eyes softened.

The child's hum shifted slightly higher, a lilting note, almost playful.

The figures beyond the mist remained where they were—silent, watching, witnesses to a choice that needed no words.

The coil didn't bind her.

It welcomed her.

And somewhere deep inside the rhythm of the mist, the stone basin, the breathing spores, Aarya heard—not in her ears, but somewhere deeper—that first wordless truth:

Memory is not what you keep.

It is what keeps you.

The coil still warm against her throat, Aarya sat back on her heels.

The mist around the basin thickened again—but this time, it was different.

It shimmered faintly at the edges, swirling faster, as if a current ran beneath it.

The child rose, spun once lightly on bare feet, and settled at Aarya's side.

The woman knelt opposite, hands resting palm-up on her knees, face calm, waiting.

The figures beyond the mist remained indistinct, yet somehow—present.

The Grove was no longer testing.

It was opening.

Aarya breathed deeply, letting the spores flood her lungs without resistance.

And the vision came.

First, a memory:

A group of settlers, decades past, hacking at the jungle's edge—axes biting into fungal-laced trunks.

Fires.

Sickness.

The silent dispersal of Gleamers into deeper groves.

She felt their grief.

Their stubborn hope.

The mist twisted again, faster.

New images surfaced—not memories.

Possibilities.

A drone overhead, its rotors slicing the air, scanning, transmitting.

BioSynth executives hunched over monitors, red dots blinking along coastlines.

Contracts signed in cold glass towers.

Gleamer blood samples cataloged, numbered, priced.

South Veyra, cleared in grids.

Spores sterilized.

Roots burned.

Aarya flinched.

The pulse at her throat thudded against her collarbone, a warning.

The mist shimmered violently—

And then softened.

Another thread wove forward:

The Grove, breathing still.

Hidden.

Remembered.

A child—different, but not—kneeling at a basin, humming.

Memory coiling forward across generations, unbroken.

If they survived.

If the silence held.

If someone chose not to betray them.

Aarya staggered slightly, hand bracing against the moss.

The woman's eyes—so steady, so knowing—held her without words.

You see it now.

The past. The threat. The choice.

The coil at her throat pulsed once more—tiny, rhythmic.

Not commanding her.

Trusting her.

She pressed her palm flat against her sternum, grounding herself.

She was not just a carrier of data anymore.

She was a carrier of memory.

And memory was a dangerous thing in the wrong hands.

Or the right one.

The evening wrapped South Veyra in velvet blue.

By the time Aarya returned to her shack, the sea beyond the trees had stilled into a vast, dark mirror. The wind had dropped, and only the slow breath of waves against the distant reef reached her ears.

She stirred a small pot of rice over the firepit outside—no spices, no extravagance. Just the simple act of heat and water and waiting.

Above her, the sky unfolded in layers—clearer here than she had ever seen from Kolkata.

The Southern Cross tilted low toward the horizon, its stars faint but certain.

To the west, the brilliant cluster of the Hyades glimmered near the setting moon, their V-shaped pattern sharp against the deeper dusk.

The Pleiades—the Seven Sisters—hung higher still, a delicate mist of light, soon to sink after them.

Near the zenith, Canopus, the great star of the south, burned steady, a lighthouse pinned in blackness.

Aarya lay back against the worn wooden boards outside the shack, arms folded behind her head, letting the smells of salt and ash weave into her hair.

She tried not to think about the retrieval team.

About BioSynth.

About the ticking clock sealed inside the silent tablet still zipped inside her pack.

Tonight was for breathing.

Tonight was for remembering what it meant to belong to earth, not to orders.

The stars blurred slightly—not from clouds, but from her own unfocused gaze—as memory seeped up, unbidden.

Kolkata | Rabindra Sarobar Lake | 23 September 2072 | Early Evening

Rohan's hand was warm against hers, his thumb tracing small circles along her knuckles.

They walked slowly along the cracked footpaths that wove through Rabindra Sarobar, the air heavy with the sharp green smell of algae and the distant smoke of street food carts setting up for the night.

He pointed across the lake, where the water caught the gold blush of a dying sun.

"Did you know," he murmured, "this lake was man-made? Dug out in the 1920s. But it's old now.

Older than half the people who live around it."

His voice dipped lower, almost reverent.

"They call it the lungs of South Kolkata.

But we choke it every day without thinking."

She remembered how his face looked then—backlit by the water, a seriousness in his features she hadn't seen often.

A seriousness she had loved without understanding fully.

He bent to pick a loose strand of wild grass, twirled it absently between his fingers.

"Even things made by hands," he said, "even cities—

they need to be remembered, or they'll forget how to breathe."

Later, they had sat on the stone steps by the lake's edge, knees brushing, his jacket around both their shoulders, the city blinking slowly to life behind them.

He had kissed her temple softly, no urgency, no hunger.

Only belonging.

Only memory.

South Veyra Island | 14 April 2075 | 20:10 IST

Aarya blinked up at the night sky.

Canopus still burned steady overhead.

The waves kept breathing against the reef.

The rice steamed in its pot, forgotten.

And somewhere inside her, old promises—half-spoken, half-kept—stirred awake.

Memory didn't vanish.

It waited.

Just like the Grove.

Just like love.

The dawn broke thin and silver across the sea.

Aarya woke slowly, the rough grain of the shack's floorboards imprinted along one cheek, the embers of last night's fire reduced to faint warmth under her palm.

The air smelled sharper than before.

Saltier.

Drier.

The scent of a wind not born from the island, but from ships far offshore.

She sat up, blinking against the low sunlight. The rice pot, now cool and half-full, stood beside her.

A few gulls circled high above, restless.

Something tugged at her chest—a familiar sensation now.

Not fear.

Not warning.

Awareness.

She rose stiffly, brushing ash from her sleeves, and walked to the edge of the treeline.

The sea glittered under the hardening light.

Far to the west—almost invisible unless you knew where to look—something moved against the water's skin.

A shadow.

No sails.

No nets.

No movement of birds above it.

Metal.

Patrol.

She touched the coil of spore-thread at her throat, feeling its tiny, steady warmth.

No hum of drones yet.

No thudding boots on the trail.

But the world she had left behind—the world she had tried, for a few nights, to silence—was already pressing against the island's skin.

She turned back to the shack, moving quickly but without panic.

She packed lightly:

- The notebook,
- The bark spiral,
- A waterskin,
- A folded length of cloth with a simple clasp—the kind Rohan had once used to bind plants gently to driftwood for rooting.

She left behind the tablet.

Left behind the satchel marked with the IICHA insignia.

Left behind the tethers that had been fraying since the moment she had set foot on South Veyra.

The Grove waited.

And so did the storm.

But for once, Aarya knew which one she belonged to.

07:11 IST

The path back into the interior felt different this morning.

The mist hadn't lifted.

If anything, it had grown heavier—pressing low against the earth, knotting itself into thicker cords that clung to the roots and ferns.

The fungal webs along the trees pulsed faintly, their usual soft green blush now edged with a pale violet shimmer.

A signal.

A warning.

The Grove knew.

Aarya moved carefully, matching her breath to the shifting rhythm of the mist.

It wasn't resistance she felt.

Not hostility.

It was preparation—like a lung filling before a long-held breath.

Even the birds were quieter.

Even the insects buzzed lower in the underbrush, huddling into folds of bark and leaf.

She caught glimpses, here and there, between the thicker mists:

- A flash of a child's bare foot vanishing into the shadows.
- A low vibration under her soles as the Grove's pulse sped up, slower than human urgency but deeper, more lasting.

She understood without needing words:

The Memory Grove was not passive.

It remembered invasion.

And it knew how to endure.

The fire pit near the basin had been swept clean, the stone polished to a dull sheen.

The woman stood waiting at the basin's edge, the child tucked beside her hip, both of them still, alert, humming so low Aarya felt it more in her sternum than in her ears.

The male Gleamer emerged from a root cluster farther back, slinging something over his shoulder—some tool or weapon shaped from vine and bone.

Other figures—silent, mist-bound—watched from behind veils of fungal curtains.

Not hiding.

Not welcoming.

Waiting.

The spores thickened around Aarya's arms, their threads brushing like curious fingers.

She crossed into the basin's circle.

The hum deepened.

Her own body responded—pulse steady, breath slow, skin vibrating gently at the places where memory and blood had first intertwined.

No orders needed shouting.

No plans needed drafting.

The island had already decided:

It would not erase itself again.

And neither would she.

07:37 IST

The woman moved first.

She stepped into the basin's shallow mist, hands open, palms upward, the coil of memory at her own throat visible now—woven deeper into her skin, pulsing faintly.

The child followed, her small frame trailing a breath of spores behind her.

The male did not join them.

He circled the grove's perimeter instead, his eyes sharp, scanning the forest beyond, where the world pressed closer with every passing hour.

Aarya understood.

This was not a ritual to be witnessed.

It was a bond to be renewed.

She stepped forward.

The mist coiled tighter around her calves, her knees, the hollow at the base of her spine.

The Grove's pulse thickened—not frantic, but deep and slow, like an ancient drum beating far below the roots.

Aarya pressed her hand once more to her throat, feeling the tiny coil of spore-thread thrum against her skin.

She knelt at the basin.

Not to study.

Not to conquer.

To remember.

To carry.

The woman reached out—not touching, not commanding—only sharing her breath, her hum, her pulse into the rising mist between them.

And Aarya breathed in answer.

The figures beyond the mist—others she had not yet spoken to, names she would never learn—lifted their heads as one.

The basin pulsed.

The mist thickened.

The Grove closed its arms around her—not as a prison, not as a refuge, but as a memory choosing its next bearer.

Aarya closed her eyes.

The world of BioSynth, of retrieval codes and silent extractions, of betrayals tucked into memos, slipped further away.

The pulse of the Grove, and of her own heart, merged into one rhythm:

Remember,

Endure,

Protect.

***

Interlude: BioSynth Internal Briefing Excerpt

Mumbai Biotech Zone 3 | BioSynth HQ | 15 April 2075 | 08:32 IST

(Restricted—Level 9: Strategic Asset Division)

Meeting Transcript

Subject: South Veyra Asset Review

Chair: NARESH KOTHARI (Exec. Director, Asset Prospecting)

Attendees: Dr. Susan Ven (Bio-Sovereignty IP), Col. Ritesh Kumar (Risk Oversight), Anirudh Sheel (PLA Liaison, Observer Status), and internal stakeholders.

KOTHARI:

Let's make this effective.

Sector E7 has still not replied on the IICHA field feed. Operative SEN, Aarya now exceeds the 72-hour survival timeframe. Our retrieval team had provided a recommended strategy yesterday, Protocol SOLACE, but this was deferred pending this meeting.

VEN:

I recommend immediate deployment. We have confirmation of bioluminescent signatures consistent with Phase IV Gleamer presence. Their biology—specifically blood immunity and spore-sensory dermis—has no comparative model in any known Southeast Asian gene pool.

KUMAR:

We're already red-flagged with the UN Biodiversity Ethics Board after the Myanmar strain breach. We need airlock chain-of-custody this time. No unsealed samples.

SHEEL (Observer):

[Note: Spoken in Mandarin-accented English]

I would suggest containment first and samples later. The opportunity for intelligence is rapidly decreasing. Our side doesn't appreciate to be delayed when it comes to strategic pathogens.

KOTHARI:

Yes, well, our side prefers profit.

Let's not forget:

The Gleamer strain isn't just resilient. It's irreplaceable. Blood shows zero autoimmune rejection.

Spore-binding proteins show full adaptivity in hostile environments.

We're not talking about curing diseases anymore.

We're talking about replacing the immune system.

Permanent immuno-design.

Field-ready resilience.

Exportable life.

VEN:

And SEN has likely already made contact. Her biological status may now be… compromised. Or enhanced.

KOTHARI:

Either way, she's secondary.

The site is the resource.

Recommend full retrieval—with lethal clearance authorized in case of resistance.

KUMAR:

I'll issue the tactical memo. Local drones will soft-scan by dusk. On-ground team can land in thirty hours if unchallenged.

KOTHARI:

Good. Wrap it.

Memo Ends.

Addendum (Encrypted – KOTHARI Only):

China wants proof of scalability. The contract isn't just for immunity. It's for control.

They want the spores that remember.

And the girl, if possible.

But not necessary.

***

Chapter 7: The Encroachment

The light had hardened.

No longer soft like dawn, no longer filtered through morning mist.

Now the sun pressed down with a white weight, and the mist had pulled back—not retreating, but recoiling, folding into the Grove's lowest hollows like breath held tight behind clenched teeth.

Aarya stood near the basin, hands loose at her sides. The moss beneath her feet felt hotter than before—drier, as though the forest floor had begun to brace itself.

The woman crouched near the fire pit, unmoving, eyes closed, fingers pressed to the earth.

The child had stopped humming.

She knelt behind a gnarled root, her small face turned toward the canopy, watching.

The male Gleamer appeared from the east, his approach faster than usual, body tense.

A long cut streaked his left forearm—fresh, glinting red-black under the sunlight that now slashed through the tree trunks at an unnatural angle.

He signed quickly, with firm motions—fewer gestures this time. Urgent.

The woman opened her eyes, nodded once.

Aarya didn't need translation.

She felt it before she heard it.

A distant whirr.

Low-frequency.

Circular.

Not bird. Not insect. Not wind.

She raised her eyes to the canopy.

The leaves above barely rustled, but something passed through the air—a metallic heat, like static before a storm.

Far above, unseen but closing, a drone was descending.

Not mapping.

Not surveying.

Marking.

She touched the coil at her throat.

Its pulse, once gentle and in sync with the Grove's breath, now beat faster, like a heart that sensed blood had entered the water.

The fungal webs around the basin began to glow again—but this time with a stutter, a shimmer of violet edge.

The Grove remembers.

It knows the sound of what comes to burn.

The child swayed.

One small hand clutched the spiral bark token at her chest, and the other pressed against her temple.

She wasn't crying. But her hum had vanished, and in its absence, the air felt sharper.

The woman moved quickly, wrapping the child's small form into a cloth sling at her hip.

Aarya stepped forward, instinct overriding protocol, science, fear.

"Let me," she whispered.

The woman looked at her—not with surprise, but with permission—and shifted the child carefully into Aarya's arms.

The child was warm. Too warm.

Her skin was damp with spore sweat, and Aarya could feel the fluttering misalignment in her breathing—like the spores in her lungs were vibrating at the wrong frequency.

The drone's sound had faded into the distance, but the damage lingered in the child's rhythm.

Spore dissonance.

Not an infection.

A rejection of what had no memory.

The woman turned and began walking—not toward the basin, not toward the ridge—but along a low-cleared trail Aarya had never seen before.

It wound between thick root systems and fallen trees crusted with ochre-colored mycelium.

The mist here was thinner, but the fungal webs along the ground grew denser, woven like rugs across the soil.

Every step released a scent she hadn't smelled before:

earth mixed with salt, crushed bone, and ash.

Older memory.

Deeper.

The child whimpered softly in her arms. Not pain. Not fear.

Fatigue.

Aarya shifted her weight, tightening her grip.

She didn't ask where they were going.

The Grove was guiding them now—not with words, not with maps, but through the slow unfurling of paths that appeared only when needed.

Ahead, the trail dropped into shadow.

The woman descended without hesitation.

And Aarya followed—with the child against her chest, and the spores in the air beginning to shift their pulse.

The trail narrowed into a hollow—roots forming an arch overhead, heavy with thick strands of bioluminescent mycelium.

The woman stooped slightly as she entered.

Aarya followed, cradling the child close, ducking beneath the living lattice that hung like braided hair from the ceiling.

The air changed immediately.

Cooler.

Denser.

Not oppressive—but rich, like air that had been used before and was still remembering how it was once breathed.

The light came not from fire or sun, but from the spores themselves—each glowing gently from within the walls, threads woven so thickly they looked like velvet pulled over stone.

A basin rested at the chamber's center, carved directly into the ground, its lip rimmed with moss the color of soot.

But what struck Aarya first wasn't the shape, or the architecture, or even the pulse she felt through the floor.

It was the silence.

Not absence.

Not stillness.

But a silence that held weight.

As if every hum, every breath, every story ever inhaled into the Grove had been collected here—compressed, stored, sleeping.

The woman knelt beside the basin and gestured for Aarya to sit.

She obeyed without hesitation.

The child stirred, moaning softly.

The woman placed her palm over the girl's chest, then dipped her other hand into a bowl carved from fungal bark. She smeared a dark salve across the child's temples and throat.

Within moments, the girl's shivering slowed.

Her breath leveled.

Her hum returned—barely audible, but present again.

Aarya exhaled slowly, realizing she had been holding her breath.

Not from fear.

From reverence.

She looked up. The woman was watching her—not with command, not with question, but with expectation.

The fungal threads along the ceiling began to shift.

Not randomly.

Patterned.

A braid.

A spiral.

A timeline woven in air.

And in the quiet, Aarya felt it:

This was not just a place of hiding.

It was a library made of blood, breath, and soil.

A living backup.

A vault for memory.

Every invasion, every silence, every grief the Grove had ever survived—

was kept here.

Waiting.

Fungal Vault | 15 April 2075 | 09:34 IST

The threads above her shifted again.

At first, they simply shimmered, as if catching a breeze that didn't exist. Then the movement became patterned—spiraling outward, the same ancient geometry the child had drawn in ash, the same one Baba had once traced with charcoal and breath.

Each strand brightened slightly, a dull amber glow moving through it like pulse-light in a vein.

Aarya blinked.

And saw.

Not with her eyes.

Not with hallucination.

But through the way memory rose through her breath, woven into the spores that now lined her throat, her lungs, her blood.

Memory Grove | 1880s, Colonial Entry | Gleamer Recollection

The scent came first—foreign cloth, oil, leather, horses.

Men with voices that cracked the air.

Shadows in khaki, dragging their boots across moss and coil.

A Gleamer boy crouched beside the very basin where Aarya now sat—his heart a drumbeat pressed against bark.

He watched the men raise fire along the forest's rim.

"*Survey for settlement,*" one said.

"*Nothing here but monkeys and rot.*"

A torch fell.

A ring of flame caught on the outer threads of the Grove.

The boy didn't scream.

He reached into the basin instead—cupped mist into his palms—and exhaled it outward.

The mist spiraled through the air, slow, deliberate.

It wrapped around the men's ankles, their weapons, their eyes.

The torch died.

And the men—forgetting why they had come—turned back to their boats by dusk.

Not frightened.

Just... misdirected.

South Veyra Island, Fungal Vault | Present

Aarya gasped.

Her palms were pressed flat against the moss.

Her breath came ragged.

The memory had passed through her—not as vision, but as function.

The Grove had not resisted with rage.

It had resisted with forgetting.

A defense made of disorientation.

A memory so deep it could unmake yours.

She looked up.

The woman had not moved.

But the pattern above them faded, slowly.

The strands quieted, returning to their resting pulse.

And Aarya understood:

What the Grove remembered, it could also remove.

That was its power.

And now, part of it lived inside her.

The child's hum had steadied.

Aarya placed a hand gently over the girl's chest. Beneath her palm, the breath now moved slow and clean, no longer fragmented by synthetic interference.

The woman met her eyes and gave a short nod—approval, or perhaps simply readiness.

They had to return.

Aarya stepped carefully out of the vault, ducking back through the root tunnel. The fungal threads brushed her shoulders like warm hair, a parting gesture from something alive.

Outside, the air had shifted again.

It was brighter.

Too bright.

The sun had climbed higher—directly overhead now, burning through the thinning canopy in sharp slashes.

She picked up her pace, rounding the basin where the ritual had taken place.

Then she stopped.

The moss was disturbed.

A wide print—a boot, deep enough to have come from a heavy heel.

Aarya crouched low.

Another footprint.

Then a third—lighter, less distinct, but angled toward the fire pit.

Her chest tightened.

She turned toward the slab of stone near the basin, where she had tucked her notebook that morning before the vault descent.

It was gone.

The slab was bare.

Only the ghost of the coil she'd laid beside it remained, an indentation of memory without form.

She rose slowly, eyes scanning the perimeter.

The male Gleamer was not in sight.

Neither were the shadowed figures beyond the mist.

Only the birds had returned—cautious, wide-winged, dipping low and circling.

And behind them, far beyond the Grove's invisible perimeter—

A low, delayed echo.

Like wind.

Or rotor.

Aarya pressed her hand to her chest, her fingertips brushing the coil at her throat.

If BioSynth had taken the notebook...

They would have not just her notes, but her drawings, her emotional logs, her spore data.

A map to the Grove's breath.

And if the male Gleamer had taken it—

Then it was either safe…

Or lost forever.

Either way, the Grove's time in hiding was ending.

The world was drawing its boundary.

And Aarya was now standing at its edge.

Grove's Edge | 15 April 2075 | 10:08 IST

She found him near the eastern rise.

The male Gleamer stood half in shadow, eyes narrowed against the sun, one hand resting on the trunk of a tree veined with deep red threads—a warning line, Aarya realized. The perimeter the Grove had drawn for itself.

Beyond that point, the forest grew quieter—not with peace, but with absence.

He did not turn as she approached.

She stopped a few paces away, close enough to see the fresh cut on his arm had dried but not been cleaned.

"Did you take it?" she asked softly.

No response.

Not a word.

Not a gesture.

Only the twitch in his jaw, a small pulse beneath his skin.

"My notebook," she said. *"The one I left by the basin."*

His eyes flicked toward her—brief, sharp.

A breeze passed between them, carrying with it the faint scent of citrus and alcohol.

Fungal suppressant.

BioSynth was closer than she thought.

He stepped forward—just once—closing the space between them.

Still no words.

But this time he raised his hand and opened it.

Inside: a folded leaf. Smooth. Unmarked. Sealed at the edges with fungal gum.

He held it out.

She hesitated.

Then took it.

Opened it.

Inside were three pages from her notebook.

Just three.

Torn cleanly.

Not destroyed.

Preserved.

Sketches of the Grove's basin.

One drawing of the spiral-bark symbol.

And a half-written note in her own handwriting:

"They breathe not to speak but to remember."

Aarya looked up.

His face was unreadable.

But behind the stillness, something coiled:

Not anger.

Not betrayal.

Caution.

"You don't trust me," she said. Not accusatory. Just truth.

He opened his mouth—but didn't speak in words.

The sound he made was low, almost sub-vocal.

A vibration, more than language.

Like a hum buried in the ribs, or the final breath before a seed splits open.

Aarya didn't know how she understood.

But she did.

Not trust.

Not rejection.

Yet.

Grove Perimeter | 15 April 2075 | 10:21 IST

The air vibrated.

Not sharply—not like before, when the drone's rotors shredded the silence—but deeper now, slower.

The mist curled tighter around the trees. The fungal webs across the forest floor began to thrum, one by one, like strings being tuned in a forgotten instrument.

Not retreat.

Not panic.

Response.

Aarya turned slowly, her feet pressing into the soft mat of moss and mycelium.

The pulse was rising.

She could feel it beneath the skin, just below the collarbone, where the spore-thread coil rested like a second heartbeat.

The child had been moved to the deeper vault.

The woman remained near the basin, kneeling, her hum barely audible—like a code stitched into the soil.

Others had emerged too.

Not crowding.

Just present.

One stood halfway up a tree's root flare, another crouched beneath the hanging coils of vine-thick spores.

All of them watching.

Not her.

The perimeter.

Something was coming.

And they weren't going to fight it with weapons.

They were going to fight it with confusion, with directionlessness, with living misdirection.

She stepped forward, closer to the Grove's edge.

"Let me go," she said. Not a question.

The male Gleamer stood nearby, unmoving.

"They're looking for me," she continued. *"They know my markers, my signals. My notebook. My tags."*

She pulled a strip of fiber from her belt pouch—the woven band Rohan had once used to bind seedlings to waterlogged wood.

She held it up, then tied it to the bark near the path.

A sign.

A decoy.

"They'll follow the wrong trail if I give it to them."

The Grove pulsed around her—not in approval or dissent.

In recognition.

She took a step beyond the red-thread warning line.

No hum stopped her.

No hands pulled her back.

Only the mist followed—spooling quietly around her ankles as she began to walk.

She would lead them wrong.

So, the memory could remain right.

Jungle Edge | 15 April 2075 | 10:38 IST

The jungle beyond the Grove felt colder.

Not in temperature—but in intent.

The moment Aarya stepped past the fungal boundary, she felt the shift.

The moss was thinner here, the trees more spaced, the fungal webs less complex—as though memory had withdrawn its reach.

But the mist still followed.

It trailed her like a shadow, slow and silver, veiling her footprints as she walked.

She moved without hesitation.

The spore-thread coil at her throat pulsed less now—not because the Grove was fading, but because it had entrusted her with a task.

Do not resist.

Do not strike.

Distract.

Confuse.

Protect.

She left tiny signs:

- A scrap of cloth snagged on a thorn.
- A leaf with fresh writing tucked into a low crevice.
- A bootprint pressed deliberately near a small clearing.

She was building a trail.

False.

Convincing.

Human.

The forest seemed to hold its breath with her.

No birdsong.

No insects.

Even the wind had stilled.

Only the faintest buzz—low, mechanical—hinted that the metal eye was still searching.

And it would find her.

She paused beside a shallow pool, its surface opaque with algae.

Kneeling, she dipped her fingers into the water, smearing mud along her forearms and neck—masking the fungal traces, dulling the warmth of the spores.

Not to erase herself.

To become bait.

The sound grew louder.

She stood.

Lifted her chin.

And walked on.

Lower Jungle Ridge | 15 April 2075 | 11:02 IST

The trees thinned.

Not cleared—just evenly spaced, unnaturally precise, as though someone had trimmed the jungle with an eye for surveillance.

Aarya slowed her pace.

She could hear it now—clearly this time.

A drone.

Low-altitude.

High-frequency.

Moving just above the canopy in slow, sweeping arcs.

She counted between pulses.

Seven seconds between passes.

She stepped into a small clearing where the light slanted hard and metallic, as if the sky had opened its eye.

She did not crouch.

Did not hide.

She simply waited.

A soft click above her—nearly inaudible.

Then a flash: infrared scan, sweeping vertically.

They have her heat signature.

Another click.

She raised her head slowly—enough for the collar of her shirt to shift, revealing a sliver of skin, mottled with fungal patterns she had not even realized had emerged.

Then stillness.

Let them see it.

Let them wonder.

Let them follow her.

One body.

One echo.

Draw them from the Grove.

She closed her eyes, letting her breath slow.

The spores in her lungs did not panic.

They pulsed.

Gently.

Steadily.

The drone moved closer.

She heard the micro-motors correct their angle—hovering just ten meters above the brush.

She opened her eyes.

Stared straight into the invisible lens.

"Come find me," she whispered.

And then turned—slowly, deliberately—into the thicker forest beyond, where no memory had yet been drawn.

Transitional Forest Zone | 15 April 2075 | 11:13 IST

She moved through the thinning jungle, her pace steady, deliberate—each step placed like punctuation.

Behind her, the Grove was silent.

Before her, the air was electric.

And within her, the question arrived—

Why not fake the data?

Why not go back to the shack, clean the logs, adjust the spore metrics, and write a quiet fiction?

She could have.

She knows that.

She could've stayed close to shore. Let the drones sweep past.

Logged decay where it didn't bloom.

Drawn fungus without eyes.

Filed harmless entries that pleased Delhi, pleased BioSynth, pleased the hungry mouths of the Party.

And no one would've known.

Except her.

Except the Grove.

Except the memory inside her blood that now hummed louder than fear.

Because silence is no longer safe.

Because what they want now isn't data.

It's blood.

It's the spores.

It's the *structure of breath itself.*

Because she's seen what forgetting looks like—

a flat lab report, a missing sketch, a mother's trembling hand tossing ash into a fire.

She remembers Baba's eyes as he watched spores rise off a petri dish like prayer.

She remembers Ma's arms shaking as she burned his work out of love.

And she remembers what it felt like

to feel the Grove's pulse

choose her.

Not to study it.

To carry it.

She crested a low ridge. The sea came into view again—gray now, metallic, watched.

She knelt behind a gnarled tree and laid a final trail mark—three small stones, spiraled.

The drone was close again.

She could hear the motors recalibrating, narrowing their cone.

She didn't move.

She let them come.

"You want the Grove," she whispered, *"but I am the Grove now."*

Memory Grove | Basin | 15 April 2075 | 11:13 IST

The child stirred.

The woman looked up.

The basin pulsed—slow and deep—its mist rising again like breath caught in memory.

And from the roots came a hum—low, ancient, thick with history.

A song.

Not of mourning.

Not of war.

A song of preparation.

The Grove had seen this before.

And this time,

it remembered how to endure.

***

Interlude: PLA Orders: Operation Specimen-V

Undisclosed Naval Vessel, Bay of Bengal

15 April 2075 | 06:42 CST (China Standard Time)

(Encrypted Transmission - Xiangwei Satellite Loop)

Classified Briefing – Vice Colonel Lin Yuwei, PLA Southern Reconnaissance Division

Status: Level 7 – Soft Intervention Protocol

Target: **Specimen-V** (Gleamer strain, South Veyra Island)

Observation Host: Republic of India (IICHA/BioSynth)

LIN YUWEI (audio):

Proceed without notifying the Indian coastal authority.

No IICHA clearance. No shared data chain.

BioSynth has compromised integrity of containment.

Extraction is now unilateral.

"Specimen-V" displays fungal traits confirmed in Myanmar 2072:

— Dermal spore symbiosis

— Immune adaptation

— Electrosensory mirroring

— Non-verbal biolinguistics

— Possible memory resonance encoding

If confirmed—this isn't folklore.

This is **sovereign biotech**.

UNIDENTIFIED OFFICER:

Sir, won't direct interference breach treaty alignment with—

LIN:

BioSynth is ours.

Fifteen percent stake.

Four shell funds.

The predictive model they use to track mycelium spread?

Written in Hangzhou.

India's "green" party is the mask.

We're the oxygen.

LIN (cont'd):

Mission outline:

- Follow drone telemetry tagged "SEN-A27"
- Log pulse variations
- Monitor thermal misalignment
- Retrieve target if viable
- Neutralize any indigenous vectors with minimal trace

No ID.

No incident.

No flag.

You don't need thanks.

You need to be first.

[Transmission auto-deletes in 30 seconds]

***

Chapter 8 – The Threshold

South Veyra Island, Outer Jungle Clearing | 15 April 2075 | 13:01 IST

The first one appeared like a mirage—blurred at the edges, shivering with heat.

Aarya stood still, her back straight, body caked in dried mud and faint fungal residue. The midday sun poured down like molten glass, and the leaves around her barely stirred.

She had reached the edge of the path she had marked with stone spirals and thread scraps.

Now she waited.

The soldier—though not quite a soldier, more logistics than combat—stepped forward through the undergrowth, visor down, mask sealed tight, a compact scanner blinking on his forearm. He was wrapped in light-reactive gear, cloth that shimmered grey-green like snake skin.

He froze when he saw her.

She saw his fingers twitch toward the comm switch on his shoulder.

Another figure followed.

Then a third.

Three in total, spreading out in a staggered line, not speaking.

BioSynth protocol.

She recognized the pattern: secure, tag, extract.

They thought she was an asset gone rogue.

Maybe they thought she was infected.

Maybe they thought she was a lead.

But none of them thought she was waiting.

That's their mistake.

Aarya raised her hands slowly. Not a surrender.

A signal.

One of them barked a clipped command—garbled under the mask.

She didn't move.

Didn't answer.

The scanner on the first agent's wrist beeped erratically.

He slapped it twice. Adjusted the frequency.

Still pulsing red.

Spores on her skin were interfering—creating ghost signatures, like heat bouncing off water.

The Grove is already inside their machines.

One of them stepped forward, pulling out a soft injector—sedative pre-load.

Aarya turned slightly, baring her neck.

Let them come close.

Let them scan.

Let them tag her.

But let them never find the Grove.

The injector hovered at her neck.

She felt the breath of the tech's glove near her skin—not warmth, exactly, but a charged stillness, like static clinging to the air before a monsoon breaks.

Then the second agent spoke:

"Scan's dirty. She's laced."

The first paused. *"External spores?"*

"No. Internal. Full bio-merge. Some kind of spore-thread activation."

He stepped back, scanner tilted toward her clavicle. The readout pulsed violet-blue, flickering. The data blurred, then reformed—like a loop glitching just out of comprehension.

"She's broadcasting."

Aarya said nothing.

But she exhaled—slow, deep, letting the spore-thread coil at her throat hum gently in the space between her lungs.

The scanner let out a high-frequency whine and blinked white.

Overload.

The Grove had not only entered her.

It was interfering with their language.

The third agent tapped his helmet.

"Command, this is Alpha Two—subject located, but signal's fractured. No visual anchor. Requesting Z-Glass clearance."

A pause.

Static hissed.

Then a new voice crackled through—cold, metallic:

"Confirmed. Proceed with Extraction. High-priority specimen.

Do not engage verbally. Quarantine on contact."

Aarya blinked once. The forest around her shimmered at the edges.

The spores near her wrists began to glow faintly—not visible unless one was looking for it.

The second agent stepped closer with a restraint band.

"Easy. You're being relocated."

Relocated.

Like a file. A pathogen. A thing.

She tilted her head slightly, the barest shift, and whispered—

"I'm already home."

The Grove responded.

Not with noise.

But with a small temperature drop. A shift in wind direction. A bloom of scent—ash, bark, heat—pressing outward like breath returning to the earth.

The scanner shorted.

One of the agents cursed.

And above them, the drone blinked red.

Unmapped.

Unaligned.

Uncertain.

The Grove was starting to speak back.

The drone stuttered overhead.

Aarya didn't look up, but she heard it—a rhythmic flutter in the rotors, off-beat, like a skipping heart. Its light shifted erratically: green to amber, then red. Then back again.

Sensor loop. Spores disrupting visual telemetry.

The agents hadn't noticed it yet.

One still circled her with the restraint band, another manually rebooted his scanner, slapping the casing with a gloved hand.

The third—the youngest—had stopped moving altogether.

He stood ten paces back, visor half-tilted, head cocked to one side.

His voice was faint.

"She's humming."

The lead turned. *"What?"*

The young man's mask shifted. *"Not her. The trees."*

Aarya turned, slowly.

His eyes were wide. His arms dropped to his sides.

The scanner on his wrist was blinking a soft violet—not alert, but entranced.

The Grove was already in his rhythm.

He'd breathed it in.

And the spores had found memory.

His pupils dilated.

"They remember," he whispered. *"They remember everything."*

The lead cursed. *"Alpha Three, mask up. Fall back. You're—"*

The drone buzzed sharply overhead, then spun sideways—as if pushed by a gust that wasn't there.

It clipped a branch.

Corrected.

Glitched again.

Then began ascending—without instruction.

The Grove wasn't fighting it.

It was unteaching it.

Aarya let her eyes fall to the soil.

Tiny threads of fungus had emerged—pale, glistening—along the ground at her feet, curling outward in spiral forms. Not random. Not decorative.

Directional.

She was being given a path.

The lead agent looked back at her, eyes hard.

"You're coming with us. Now."

But even he sounded less certain.

Like the air itself had grown too heavy to carry intent.

Aarya took one step backward.

The fungus glowed.

Aarya turned slowly and walked.

She didn't run.

She didn't look back.

Behind her, the agents hesitated only a moment—just long enough for her breath to align with the spores rising off the soil, curling through the light like mist with intention.

Then the command snapped:

"Follow her. Move."

Boots crunched behind her.

Three sets. Uneven.

She led them northeast—not toward the Grove, not toward the vault, but toward the spiral forest, where the trees grew in recursive circles and no sound carried straight.

The Grove was drawing with her—misting deliberately, softening footprints, shifting scent trails across the wind.

She stepped through an arch of banyan roots.

The first agent followed.

Then the second.

The third—Alpha Three—stumbled.

He paused mid-step, glancing at the moss beneath his boot.

"We've been here," he muttered.

The lead hissed, *"No, we haven't. Keep moving."*

But Aarya had seen it too.

A loop.

The terrain had folded.

The Grove had created a memory knot—a living topology that redirected perception.

You think you're pursuing.

But you are walking in the story it wants you to forget.

Aarya exhaled through her nose. The spores responded, dimming slightly around her ankles.

The scanner behind her chirped again.

"Target visual lost. Subject phasing."

Phasing.

They were losing her signal—not physically, but perceptually.

The agent closest to her broke rank—rushing forward, trying to close the gap.

Aarya didn't resist.

She led him deeper.

To where the air thickened.

To where the stories had no edge.

To where even sunlight doubled back on itself.

This was the Grove's gift: *Not to hide her.*

But to unmap the world around her.

The first agent stopped.

His boots sank an inch into the moss, but he didn't notice.

His head turned slightly, then again—faster this time. His visor read nothing.

His scanner was dead.

Only the faint red LED blinked against his wrist like a heartbeat out of time.

"I just… passed this."

His voice cracked in his own earpiece.

The second agent called back, *"What?"*

But the first agent turned in a full circle now—breathing hard.

"The stone spiral. She marked this already. We looped."

He tapped his chest.

"Where's North?"

No reply.

He looked down.

The moss at his feet had grown, visibly, in the last minute.

Spore acceleration. Time slippage.

He blinked.

Something flickered.

For half a second, the moss wasn't moss.

It was a red carpet.

Another blink.

The trees were steel beams.

A voice yelling orders—not in this language.

Memory Echo: 1970s, Jungle Suppression Unit, Northeast India

A soldier.

Lost.

Breathing into a radio that only hissed.

Swearing in Mandarin.

Blood on his boot.

Wrong map.

Wrong war.

South Veyra, Present

The agent fell to his knees.

"She's—inside," he gasped. *"She's inside the terrain."*

The lead agent froze now too, his head snapping to the canopy.

He tapped into HQ—BioSynth Mumbai.

"Team Bravo. We've got… anomalous spatial interference. Memory terrain active. Request protocol upgrade. This is not a normal extraction."

Silence.

The line crackled.

Then a voice answered—not Indian, not BioSynth internal.

"Observe only. Do not breach perimeter. The subject is not primary."

The agent's eyes narrowed.

"What? This is Site E7—who the hell—?"

Click.

The line dropped.

Aarya, hidden in the spiraled grove, took one slow breath.

They were beginning to fracture.

And the Grove?

It was only just starting to speak.

The air grew thick.

Not hotter. Not heavier.

Just... layered.

Like time had folded over itself and was pressing back through every breath.

Aarya crouched low behind a root coil, her eyes trained on the clearing where the three agents stood—no longer a team, but a scatter of isolated men, each surrounded by his own echo.

The youngest, Alpha Three, had taken off his helmet.

His eyes were glassy, wide.

"They said we'd land. Then scan. Then sleep."

"Alpha Three," the lead snapped. *"Focus. We're twenty minutes in, tops."*

But the young man didn't blink.

He stared upward, his mouth slack.

"I saw my mother. Just now. At the basin."

The second agent turned. *"What basin?"*

Alpha Three shook his head slowly, the skin at his neck gleaming with sweat and a thin shimmer of spore-dust.

"She was drawing in the mud. Spirals. Humming."

The lead lifted his rifle—not to shoot, but to ground himself.

A tool in the hand. Something fixed. Something named.

"Shut up. All of you. We are pulling out."

But no one moved.

The drone above circled again—its path now jerky, as if the sky itself had become unsure of its gravity.

One final flash—

Memory Echo: 1960s, Forest Perimeter, Sino-Indian Border

A man with a rifle.

Lost in terrain that shifts beneath his boots.

His radio sputters with a woman's voice—except there are no women in his unit.

He puts the barrel to the earth.

Soil will remember where I fall, he thinks.

South Veyra, Present

The youngest agent dropped to one knee, not in pain, but in confusion.

"It's not her we're tracking," he whispered.

"It's ourselves."

Aarya felt the hum begin to rise.

This time it wasn't hers.

The Grove was speaking now.

Not to her.

To them.

***

Interlude: Whistle in the Lab

Port Aurora Research Base | 15 April 2075 | 17:10 IST

Internal Access Level: Breached | Log Status: Flagged

Dr. Anjana Rao sat alone at Terminal 6C, the lab dim except for the sterile light of her screen. Rain lashed at the shack's iron roof like it meant to peel the whole place back.

A faint fungal trace pulsed on her readout.

"Immune signal: non-human adaptive. Resistance markers present. Neuro-electrical convergence abnormal."

Location: S. Veyra, Basin Sector.

Source: BioSynth Feed Crossover: Unverified Drone Packet 27-B.

Anjana exhaled.

This wasn't soil contamination.

This was biology rewriting itself.

She tabbed open a private thread—encrypted, unstable—linked to a third-party news node in Bangalore.

Typed slowly:

"Not lab-grown. Sentient immune ecology. They knew before the project began. This is more than spores."

She attached the anonymized drone extract.

A screenshot of the metabolite sequence.

A half-corrupted file labeled "ASen_Field9"—Aarya's mark. Not for anyone else. But Anjana saw it.

Clicked **Send.**

It blinked once—Failed.

She tried again.

Nothing.

Behind her, the door hissed.

She froze.

"Long night, Doctor?"

She turned. Dr. Kiran Malik—BioSynth liaison, unflinching, voice smooth as acetate.

"We monitor outbound packets, of course," he added. *"Company protocol. You understand."*

Anjana said nothing.

"You're smart," he continued. *"Don't let that become a liability."*

"People are watching South Veyra."

"That's exactly why we don't need another martyr."

He stepped closer.

"We don't publish memory, Dr. Rao.

We bury it."

Then he left.

Quiet as mold.

Anjana sat very still.

Outside, the rain poured like the island was trying to speak in water.

Inside, the screen went black.

No logs.

No evidence.

Only the faint scent of fungal salt still on her hands.

***

Chapter 9 – The Return Signal

Port Aurora | 15 April 2075 | 18:40 IST

The server room was empty except for the sound of fans—whirring like old wings. Anjana Bose sat on a crate of defunct bioscanners, her IICHA-issued tablet balanced on her knees.

The door behind her was barred shut with a janitor's mop. A glowing "cleaning" sign blinked lazily in the corridor.

The signal had first appeared that morning—encoded in fungal decay reports from South Veyra. Buried in metadata: a biometric hash she recognized instantly.

Aarya Sen.

Still alive. Still trying.

Anjana adjusted her glasses. Her palms were damp.

"Just one bounce," she whispered. *"Just one safe bounce."*

She opened a forbidden tunnel—legacy IICHA mesh routes from the early Andaman surveillance days. Deprecated after the 2062 shutdown. Unstable. Untraceable.

Lines of code bloomed across the screen. Packet routing. Compression. Redirect through a defunct marine buoy.

Her voice cracked slightly as she recorded.

"Aarya… it's Anjana. We haven't stopped looking. I've rerouted this through Cold Net Bunker 9—BioSynth won't see it unless they're still scraping pre-63 structures, which I doubt. If you're out there—

...just reply. Anything."

She attached a memory fragment—Aarya's last voice note from weeks ago. The one where she whispered, *"I won't forget."*

Anjana watched the transmission bar crawl forward like a slug across glass.

She didn't know if it reached.

But something inside her—something fungal and furious—told her it had to.

Kolkata | 15 April 2075 | 20:52 IST

Rohan leaned against the weather-stained railing of his terrace, a mug of untouched tea cooling in his hand. The monsoon was late, but the air already smelled like wet books.

He had written letters. Filed inquiries. Mailed voice requests to IICHA—some as a citizen, some as a registered next of kin. All returned unread. *"Insufficient clearance." "Subject unlisted."*

Tonight, he didn't write.

He spoke, into a small dictaphone his students had given him on his last birthday. The red light blinked.

"You said the spores remember, Aarya. So remember me.

You once told me that fungi don't forget what the forest teaches them.

So if you're inside something now—if something's growing around you—

Let it carry my voice."

He paused. You could hear the tram bells echoing faintly from Shyambazar.

"Come home. That's all I want. Not medals. Not marvels. Just... you back.

Remember that pond? That stupid picnic where I fell asleep in the grass?

That's the day I knew."

He clicked off the recorder.

He didn't know how sound travelled between islands and machines and dreams. But he believed spores carried memory. And if they carried it, they might also deliver it.

He turned the dictaphone toward the stars.

The blinking red light was steady. Then it faded.

South Veyra, Grove Threshold Site 3 | 16 April 2075 | 06:25 IST

The morning air was trembling with a strange clarity, as if the storm that had passed in the night had wrung clean not just the forest, but her skin. The grove whispered in chords. Not sound, not speech, but patterns: rising-falling frequencies that moved through Aarya's body like breath. Since dawn, she had been tuning the transmitter—no longer the clunky biosensor slab it had once been, but now webbed with restructured spore veins and resonance moss.

She worked slowly, deliberately. The Grove was listening, responding. Every component—fungal threads harvested from the Memory Grove, polished coral transducers from the reef, the mycelial nodules grown in the soil beneath her shack—hummed with potential. It was no longer a machine. It was an instrument of layered intent.

Aarya unrolled the copper-fiber mesh, letting her fingers trace each filament. She hummed softly. Not a melody, exactly—more an invocation. *"Let them hear, but not take. Let them know, but not unmake."* The phrase had come to her the night before, in that half-sleep state where the Grove sometimes sent her echoes of memories not her own.

The signal couldn't be straightforward. A clean ping, a direct frequency—BioSynth or the PLA would trace it, isolate it, sterilize it. She had to bury it in contradiction: signal as camouflage, truth as enigma.

So she coded it in layers—

Bioacoustic loops—fragments of insect-wing flutter from the deep forest, layered with harmonic intervals she'd extracted from Gleamer chants.

Spore pulses—oscillating spores that mimicked cosmic microwave background echoes; noise to some, but not to all.

Memory folds—encrypted sequences structured from her own neural imprint, stored in a dormant strand of her earlier logs. Rohan's voice was embedded in one. So was Ma's. Baba's sketches, those that once survived.

She didn't even know what part of this would be received. But that wasn't the point.

The transmitter was pulsing faintly now, calibrated to rhythms of the root systems beneath the Grove. It would take another hour before it could push its first echo out across the ridges, past the PLA drones and comms fences, toward orbit.

And somewhere—beyond the breach and noise—Aarya felt it. A pull.

Not just the Grove's call.

But something... someone... trying to call back.

Not a full message. Not even words.

Just a brief alignment of longing.

A heartbeat she couldn't trace.

Yet.

Aarya sealed the final sheath of mycelial wrap over the copper lattice. Her hands, though steady, tingled with a faint electric hum—the kind she used to feel after hours in Baba's lab, when circuits and spores blurred into one.

She whispered to the transmitter. Not in words. Just breath. Presence. Consent.

Then she placed her palm against the soft fungal core.

Thum.

The signal bloomed.

Not loud. Not bright. But vast.

A silent burst that rippled through the grove floor, climbed the trunks, and threaded the canopy with iridescent threads— barely visible in the fading light. The leaves turned faintly phosphorescent, reacting to the pulse like sea algae under moonlight.

Inside the transmitter, spore matrices vibrated into motion. Aarya watched the harmonic overlays begin to loop—a cascade of encoded frequencies laced with memory clusters, biological entropy, and acoustic mimicry.

And then—interference.

A jagged flicker.

Like static—but organic.

The pulse warped. A sharp distortion surged through the moss lining. The bioacoustic feed backtracked—looped unexpectedly—then split into two conflicting threads.

Aarya blinked.

She hadn't programmed that.

One stream continued as she had designed: cryptic, recursive, cloaked.

But the second…

It was cleaner. Narrower.

Almost as if it recognized something.

As if it were responding.

She leaned in. Tuned the lateral receptor node.

A new waveform emerged. Not hers.

A voice. Not full. But real.

"...Aarya... this is...attempt... back-channel port signal... repeat... not secure..."

She staggered backward.

The voice was distorted, but not alien.

Anjana.

At the same time, another signal spiked. Fainter. Male.

"...Kolkata... if this reaches... Rohan..."

Aarya froze. The air felt thick. The Grove itself stilled, listening.

The transmitter was not just sending anymore.

It had become a junction.

A bleeding conduit.

Between her, the Grove, and something reaching across from the far edge of the human network.

She steadied her breath.

"This wasn't supposed to happen," she whispered.

But somewhere inside her, something disagreed.

Maybe this was exactly what was supposed to happen.

South Veyra Grove, Inner Mycelial Node| 16 April 2075 | 08:47 IST

The transmitter hummed—not a machine's whirr, but something older. Older than language. It pulsed in cycles, woven from loops of memory-encoded spores, their filaments nested like recursive fractals of moss and thought.

Aarya crouched beside the moss-cradle, where the mycelial node had fused with the biotransmitter. It looked almost like a cradle-heart—pale glisten of wet rootlets, soft undulation of air where spores gathered. She had never seen the Grove respond like this. The spore-lattice blinked in rhythm with her own breath.

Then—distortion.

The pulse staggered. A sharp feedback skidded through the node, and Aarya fell back, her hand to her head.

zzchhhh—No. She's not in range. Loop again. Manual override? This is Anjana Bose, Level 4 Research—override initiated—

The voice splintered into static. Aarya blinked, disoriented. It wasn't coming from the transmitter's relay—it was vibrating in the fungi around her.

She crawled closer, her heart pounding. Was this...?

Rohan Sen. Archive 02121B. Urgent request. IICHA records show your signal signature—Is she still alive? Is Aarya Sen alive?

That one felt like fire—like being touched through a dream.

She whispered, *"Rohan... is this you?"*

No answer. Only a wash of silence, like someone had spoken across a chasm and was waiting, breathless.

Her hands hovered over the interface. She remembered tuning radio knobs with Baba as a child—how they'd wait for faint voices to crackle through static. Now, the Grove was her antenna, and memory itself was the dial.

The signal flexed again. This time, clearer.

"...South... hear... this... not safe... find...you..."

Her breath caught. Not just a message. A search. Rohan— was trying to locate her.

The Grove stirred. Threads shifted beneath her, as if the mycelial network had understood. Not just biological resonance. It was recognition.

But the signal was fragile, like a silk bridge spanning a chasm of noise. It could collapse. Or lead someone dangerous.

She looked around the chamber—the bloomlight dimmed, the spore strands pulsed in cautionary orange. The Grove was listening too.

Aarya reached toward the response node.

One signal out.

One signal back.

And with it, a choice.

The Grove stirred, not in sound—but in mood.

Fungal lattice gently contracted. Filament clusters pulled inward, as if bracing. Around Aarya, the bloomlight shifted to a deep ochre—warning, yes, but not refusal. The Grove was not halting her. It was asking her to consider.

A response node unfurled. Coated in slick velvet hyphae, it glowed a hesitant blue.

"If you speak back," the Grove seemed to hum, *"the world may follow your voice."*

Aarya sat cross-legged, fingers just above the node, eyes fixed on the bioluminescent rhythm across the chamber walls. It pulsed like a slow breath.

She whispered:

"I can just keep quiet. I can disappear. Let them think I'm gone."

But even she didn't believe it.

The signal had not come from nowhere.

It had arrived wrapped in recognition.

A voice from home, not a recall from IICHA or a directive from BioSynth, but a reaching—a plea.

"You are not lost. You are loved. Come back."

She saw again that dream from her fever days—the house in Shyambazar, the silhouette of Rohan at the balcony, a warm kitchen filled with quiet laughter. It had felt like memory… or premonition.

And now, the signal tethered that vision to something real.

But another whisper followed—not Rohan's.

"If you leave the Grove unguarded... they will come."

The Grove wasn't demanding her silence. It was offering a test of fidelity:

To connection, yes.

But also to protection.

She placed her hand just above the node, feeling the soft hum beneath.

Could she answer without revealing?

Could she leave a trail of ambiguity—complexity—just enough for Rohan to find her, but too dense for machines to decode?

The Grove didn't answer.

But it didn't stop her either.

The Grove allowed her breath. No alarms, no tremors. Just that quiet, complex approval—like a forest leaning in.

Aarya reached for her field tools—not metal, not glass, but the bio-interfacing kit the Grove had half-grown, half-taught her to use. Mycelial threads blinked in sleep-mode, coiled like wet nerves across her palm. She connected the first filament to the hypha-node and whispered, "Memory first."

From her pocket, she took the fragment of Baba's fungal sketch she had saved years ago—the one Ma hadn't found, hadn't burned. A spiral, feathered and impossibly delicate, like a spore fractal dreaming of wind.

She pulsed it into the Grove.

The walls changed. The lattice lit up in amber hues. It wasn't just absorbing the sketch—it was remembering her memory of it.

Then came the second layer: language, but fractured.

Not full coordinates. Not names. Just a map of emotions disguised as data.

A mycelial poem of displacement.

She coded them in:

The rhythm of Jorasanko evenings.

The taste of gondhoraj on fingers in the monsoon.

The static of Rohan's old radio in the Sarobar date memory.

Each one turned into bioacoustic ripples.

Each pulse—not a message, but a feeling.

The Grove responded with symbiosis. It added its own memory-harmonics:

The death of a centipede.

The sigh of a banyan under lightning.

The joy of a Gleamer's hand tracing bark at night.

And then, Aarya began weaving the false path.

A trail that led eastward—toward old PLA coordinates, already collapsed by erosion. She embedded decoys—glow patterns mimicking Gleamer vocal structures, but subtly wrong. To the untrained ear, it would seem promising. To those who didn't listen deeply, it would sound like truth.

But to Rohan, or Anjana—people who knew her, people who loved her—the real signal would hum just beneath.

A layered offering:

Love + Misdirection.

Hope + Defense.

The node flared green. The mycelial loops tightened.

And somewhere, far above, the Grove began to broadcast.

Port Aurora, Communications Deck – Level 3 | 16 April 2075 | 09:10 IST

"Ma'am, we have an emergent spike on Relay Track 19."

Anjana Bose dropped her coffee. The tin cup clanged against the console frame as she spun toward the screen. Her assistant, the junior comms tech, looked pale.

"Show me."

He tapped the feed. A bloom of data—erratic, non-linear, too rhythmic to be random—was unraveling across the lower bandwidth tiers.

Not encrypted.

Not hostile.

Not standard.

The signal trembled like breath.

Not words—tones. Memory echoes.

Like something human buried in a living thing.

Anjana stared at the waveform, then cross-referenced the frequency metadata. A flicker of a call-tag embedded in one of the deeper threads.

Origin: South Veyra. Provisional Node 7-G.

User fragment: …aryaS_n…

Trace: IICHA Field Agent #SEN-07

Her breath caught.

It was Aarya.

Not dead. Not missing.

Broadcasting.

"Archive the full stream," she ordered, voice tight. *"Lock it to my terminal. No cross-department sync. Understood?"*

"But this is tagged as biofield protocol," the tech mumbled. *"Shouldn't we—"*

"No sync." Her tone left no room for debate. *"Run a passively shadowed relay to gridpoint S4. Don't leave fingerprints."*

Behind her, the port's massive aerial dishes began to swivel, hunting for stable reverb. Already the network was echoing back partial signatures—enough for a whisper trail.

But Anjana wasn't smiling.

She'd seen this before.

Signals like these didn't just carry content.

They lured.

And someone else in the port was already watching.

South Veyra Grove, Observation Deck Near Node 7-G | 16 April 2075 | 09:32 IST

Aarya stood barefoot on the moss-draped overhang above the Grove's node cluster, eyes half-closed, body still humming from the signal's release.

She had felt it move—not just through the transmitter, but through the ground, the air, the memory-layered mycelium that spiraled through South Veyra like a living archive. The spores hadn't reacted violently, nor had they retreated. Instead, they'd tuned, like a forest exhaling in harmony.

A low, warbling resonance—almost like a question—echoed faintly back through her earpiece.

Not from IICHA.

Not from any orbital repeater.

Not even human.

She turned. From the treeline, a soft figure emerged—cloaked in the iridescent shawl of Gleamer fiber. She recognized the presence: not Irun, but the one called Ava-kin, who often moved silently during observation cycles.

Ava-kin didn't speak. Instead, they raised a hand, fingers stained with mycoblue. Then slowly pointed upward.

Aarya looked.

The canopy parted above the Grove's dome. Shafts of sunlight filtered down in faint golden beams. But beyond that—farther—something was blinking in a pulse-matched rhythm.

A drone.

High-altitude. Covert.

Not IICHA standard.

She felt the breath in her lungs pause.

"Someone's listening," she whispered.

Ava-kin nodded once, slowly. Then did something unexpected—walked up beside her, and in one fluid motion, marked her forehead with a smear of bioresin from their fingers. It shimmered faintly, and she felt a mild heat surge into her skin.

A glyph. A shield. A memory-knot. She didn't know yet.

But the moment Ava-kin stepped back, the low crackle of radio interference fluttered again through her pack.

And Rohan's voice, faint, scratched and filtered—

"Aarya…? If you can hear this—please—come back. I know. I know everything now."

The edges of her vision swam. The air thickened. She knelt.

And the Grove pulsed beneath her, listening, remembering, and responding.

BioSynth Surveillance Array – Orbital Relay Deck 04 | 16 April 2075 | 10:08 IST

"Ma'am. We've got a live anomaly breaching the node screen."

The voice came from deep inside the control pit—sharp, clinical. Director Siang didn't glance up from her data tablet, but the edge of her mouth twitched. *"Source?"*

"South Veyra. Low-band composite. It's… organic."

She turned now. *"Show me the lattice."*

A spiral unfolded on the holo-display above the relay deck—a constantly shifting, almost fractal transmission, nested in what looked like natural structure: like neural folds, fungal networks, sonic maps. Impossible, but precise.

It wasn't just data.

It was design.

"Someone's embedded memory logic in a sporefield," whispered the junior analyst beside her. *"That's not just environmental noise. It's... intended. It wants to be received."*

Siang's eyes narrowed. She zoomed in.

Across the signal clusters, thin pulses of human vocal fragments appeared—stuttered, layered, old and new. A name tagged itself twice.

Aarya Sen.

She muttered, *"I thought she was dead."*

The algorithm had already begun stripping the signal. They'd have something parsed and compartmentalized within the hour. But she knew that was only part of it.

"Alert Data Extraction. And move Specimen Retrieval to Stage 3," she said.

The analyst looked up, hesitant. *"But we haven't isolated the origin node. We'd risk breaching the—"*

"She's already breached us," Siang said coolly. *"Now let's see if the rest of her has something worth buying."*

The transmission pulsed again.

And somewhere inside its folds—buried deep in fungal code and fading dream-memory—was a glimpse of a Grove, untouched. Unyielding.

And something else: a choice, waiting to be misunderstood.

The grove hums—its resonance different now, edges strained. The mycelial lattice shivers faintly under Aarya's hand as if it too had overheard something.

She adjusts the tuning fork at the center of the transmitter. Her own voice—threaded into the hybrid signal—echoes back to her in broken tones. Faint, haunting, like listening to her own thoughts recorded by someone else.

"…degrade the sporefield to confuse extractors. Modulate the memory pulse to mimic environmental drift... Send no pattern twice."

She whispers it like a chant, barely aware she's doing it. Her fingers move instinctively, adapting to the Grove's feedback, tightening the signal into non-repeating loops. She isn't sending a message anymore. She's weaving a riddle of emotion, memory, and resistance—a fungus-coded ghost meant to confound every machine that tries to trap it.

Then—

A pulse.

Her breath catches. Not from her transmitter this time.

From outside.

A reply.

She leans close to the receiver node as a weak, garbled frequency climbs into audibility. Then, from static, a voice. Familiar, hoarse, insistent:

"Aarya... I don't know if this will reach you... I'm still trying every channel. Anjana said there might be a pattern. If you're alive... just— just hold on. I'm coming."

Her eyes widen. Rohan.

"They've locked the South Veyra report. But people are listening, Ary. They know you didn't run. They know IICHA sent you in."

The message degrades—scrambling in bursts of bio-interference—but his final words come through with uncanny clarity:

"If you're still in the forest, don't stay silent. Leave a mark. I'll find it. I swear."

Aarya's hand trembles slightly on the receiver.

Leave a mark.

He'd understood. Without knowing anything about spores or signals or the Grove's secret language, he still knew: she wouldn't vanish quietly.

The Grove seems to exhale beside her. The spores thicken in the air.

Aarya closes her eyes, lets the tears fall silently—not out of grief, but from a sudden, breathless clarity.

She is not lost.

Not alone.

And not done.

Aarya leans back from the receiver, pulse still trembling with the echo of Rohan's voice.

She doesn't answer immediately. Not yet.

Instead, she reaches into her satchel and pulls out the weatherworn sketchbook—the one from Baba's old notes, which she'd secretly reconstructed over the years. The paper smells faintly of mycelium now. The graphite lines warped slightly from the jungle humidity. But the sketches remain: spores in swirl, stalks shaped like cathedral arches, gleaming eyes that looked almost human.

Her father had once whispered that fungi remember. That no memory is ever lost—only misfiled in the rootwork of the world.

So, she does the unthinkable: she tears a page.

The Grove shivers.

She places it in the input slit of the transmitter's biocryptic module. Then she removes her gloves.

She lays her bare palm on the soft mycelium, breathing deeply.

"One memory," she whispers. *"That no extractor can decode."*

She doesn't send data.

She sends a moment.

Rabindra Sarobar, five years ago.

She and Rohan in the blue-streaked dusk, sitting on the water's edge. The lake catching the city's neon bloom. Rohan, rambling about Tagore and the colonial history of the park, about how the lake was built for both escape and performance.

And then: silence. The good kind.

The kind that feels like a held breath before a kiss.

She embeds that silence. The pause. The air between his words.

Not the kiss itself—she'd never tell the Grove that.

But the moment before. The possibility.

That's what she transmits.

The Grove reacts gently, as if reverently. Threads glow blue for the first time.

And just before the final pulse leaves the node, she speaks:

"For anyone listening… this is the part they never find.

The thing you loved before you were asked to choose."

A slow green flicker blinks from the receiver.

Signal Sent.

Rohan Sen: Waiting Room 12D, IICHA Communications Wing, Kolkata HQ | 17 April 2075 | 13:15 IST

The tea had gone cold.

Rohan held the paper cup anyway—its warmth now memory more than sensation. The corridor beyond the frosted glass pulsed with corridor lights and silence. A government-issued stillness. Polished, indirect, and prolonged.

He'd already sent three follow-ups to his request. *Status: Awaiting internal routing.* No direct line to South Veyra. Not without *"appropriate clearance."* Not without a *"legally verified familial claim."*

"And you're not married to her, are you?" the receptionist had asked earlier, with an apologetic shrug.

"No," he'd said.

Not anymore. Not yet.

But that wasn't the point. He knew she was out there. And more than that—something had arrived in the signal burst he'd intercepted through a retired listening terminal at the university's bioacoustics lab. A pulse. A shimmer. It wasn't music. It wasn't data. It was hers.

That night, he'd stayed up threading what little he'd captured through old fungal encoding filters Arun Sen once used—filters he'd reverse-engineered himself during his doctoral work. A glitch spiraled open. A voiceprint? A memory-fragment? Or just hope trying to imitate clarity?

Now, he was here. In a government wing that still hadn't fixed its peeling ceiling tiles.

Another door opened somewhere. A man with a badge passed, not even glancing at him.

Rohan tapped open his notes again:

"Phase-drift signature aligns with known Veyra Grove resonance model."

"Message fragment includes partial Bengali syntax. Possibly Aarya's voice."

"Attempt secure relay via secondary trans-basin channel."

He couldn't prove anything. Not to them.

But he didn't need to.

Rohan wasn't trying to save the world. He was just trying to reach her.

And if no one would send a message back?

Then maybe he'd find a way to go himself.

South Veyra Grove, Inner Mycelial Node | 17 April 2075 | 21:52 IST

The air felt thinner tonight, not with a lack of oxygen, but with the heaviness of something else—connection. Like the world was suddenly a fabric stretched taut between distant points.

Aarya crouched over the bio-organic transmitter, its filaments twitching gently, now attuned to her biochemistry. The pulse had shifted again. It wasn't random anymore. It was rhythmic, almost conversational.

She traced a glowing line of mycelium with her finger. *"If you're listening... if you're really trying..."* she whispered into the spores. *"Then don't stop."*

The Grove responded—not with words, but with a dim light trembling through its neural web. The internal bioluminescence was faster tonight, more eager, as if stirred by the contact.

And then, the next burst arrived.

Not data.

Not command codes.

But something else.

Aarya leaned closer to the pod. Within the spore-glass, a faint waveform shimmered. It wasn't from her. It wasn't from the Grove.

It was outside.

Static. Then… a modulated hum. Then…

"…Aarya. If this reaches you… I found something in your father's notes. The filters. The old grove models. You were right. I'm still here."

Aarya's breath caught. The Grove pulsed again, this time amplifying the signal into spatial resonance. The voice was warped—but unmistakable.

Rohan.

She backed away, hand trembling. A wave of heat coursed through her—confusion, joy, terror.

The whisper escaped her lips before she could stop it:

"Rohan… is this you?"

She felt the Grove slow its rhythm. As if listening too.

She sat down, stunned, pressed a hand to her temple, the other still gripping the edge of the transmitter.

Was she hallucinating? Fevered again? The earlier visions—their life, the lake, the marriage that never happened… Were they visions because of this? Were they echoes of what could still be?

She stared into the core of the fungal node pulsing softly before her.

No.

She wasn't imagining it.

This was real.

And someone out there was reaching back.

Aarya exhaled sharply.

"Okay," she whispered. *"Let's build this bridge."*

She began reconfiguring the signal pulse, splicing in one of her father's resonance curves. As she worked, she didn't even notice the Grove slowly adapting, mimicking her cadence, rethreading its own language into the bridge.

The pulse was no longer hers alone.

Aarya stared at the console—if one could call it that—a hollowed myco-capsule stitched with copper-bark thread and flecks of bioalloy, its membrane responding to breath, skin, thought. But what truly answered was neither silicon nor cell, but something stranger: the Grove had begun composing.

At first it mirrored her inputs, almost shy. Then, with eerie grace, it took over, not interrupting but echoing, evolving the resonance pattern she had seeded.

Phrases spliced with rhythm.

Data knots pulsing with embedded memory.

Even silence, measured, as if imbued with intent.

Aarya fed it more—more of Baba's sketches, his old signal maps drawn on worn graph paper; she vocalized syllables Rohan used in his theoretical language experiments at Jadavpur. She opened herself fully to it, surrendering not control, but collaboration.

The Grove listened.

And then it began to suggest.

Tiny surges in the bioacoustic frequencies hinted at code-shifts—not arbitrary, but laden with structure. She recognized the recursion: a loop from her own neuro-imprint, harvested during her fever. Somewhere between memory and fungus, her brain's electrical trace had imprinted itself into the living network.

"Wait…" she whispered, backing from the node. "You… you're learning me."

The Grove pulsed, slow and dim—consent, not coercion.

Not domination.

Reciprocity.

It was impossible to separate her thoughts from the network anymore. The signal being shaped now was not simply biological or computational—it was personal. A form of emotive logic, native neither to humans nor machines.

She played a tone—an ancient raag her Baba used to play during monsoon evenings in Shyambazar. The Grove caught it mid-air, warped it, and returned it as an envelope of data. She felt the tears rise in her throat, unbidden.

Somewhere, far off, something stirred in response.

A blip.

Another return pulse. Faint, cracked.

But carrying her own signal, looped back with a distortion signature not native to South Veyra.

A listening point.

A station.

Someone was replying.

Aarya looked up, her breath ragged.

The Grove continued humming beside her—sleepless, sprawling, and now aligned.

For the first time, it felt like a mind beside hers.

Not Gleamer.

Not human.

Not machine.

Something else.

Together, they were composing a signal so complex no extractor could fake it—

But someone who felt could follow.

And someone was.

Low-Orbit Quantum Surveillance Array – Node 7B, above Bay of Bengal | 16 April 2075 | 20:12 IST

For hours the array had skimmed silence. Beneath the belly of clouds, South Veyra's lush coastlines glowed faintly with solar bounce-back, and the Grove's inner canopy returned no anomalous signals—until now.

A narrow pulse had slipped through the quantum mesh. Not a burst. Not data. Not language. Something stranger—nonlinear. Recursive. The algorithm couldn't map it in time. It looped through spore-like cadence, ambient harmonics, and deepwave chirality—like a memory dreaming of itself.

Within the floating console station, the surveillance AI flagged it with yellow alert. The technician assigned—a sleepy-eyed junior analyst named Mikhail Sundaram—blinked at the screen as it folded and refracted.

"Artifact 7B-A-Delta… unknown origin. Non-state. Partial organic signature?"

His fingers hesitated. Then typed:

Run reverse vector trace.

Filter through Veyra relay.

Cross-check IICHA protocol overlaps.

No match.

Instead, the terminal shimmered, and for half a second, the display rendered a shape. Not a diagram. A pattern. Fungal. Fractal. Half-formed. Mikhail leaned closer. It seemed to breathe.

Then it was gone.

Downlink error. Reboot engaged.

But the system had already copied the loop and transmitted it—along unauthorized lines, toward Port Aurora, where PLA command protocols were buried under IICHA's official stack.

And somewhere beyond, deep in a lab that had once synthesized the earliest Gleamer-skin polymers, a neural-net subsystem paused its learning sequence. The old name echoed:

Sen. Aarya Sen.

Aarya's hands hover over the curved shell of the transmitter—grown now into a pale, throbbing fruit of the Grove. The membrane pulses faintly beneath her palms, syncing to the tempo of her breath, her thoughts, her memory. The Grove no longer resists her; it listens.

She inhales deeply, her fingers tightening around a slender strand of mycelial vein, coaxing it into circuit. *"Let this be enough,"* she whispers.

Around her, the chamber lights with an eerie, gentle hum—bioacoustic harmonics resonating from the spore lattice. Above, the canopy opens slightly, revealing a filtered dawn sky, dusted in mauve.

The return signal is not a broadcast.

It is a release.

From the Grove's memory core, loops of embedded dreams—echoes of touch, heat, and story—spiral outward. Embedded with quantum-temporal distortions that confuse mechanical extractions. Wrapped in glyphs only the Grove remembers how to read. Each signal strand is a contradiction, a koan, a ciphered act of resistance. A trail, not of bread crumbs—but of spores. Each one impossible to follow without becoming part of the forest.

Aarya adds her own final layer: a single pulse of emotional resonance. She thinks of Rohan. Of Ma. Of Baba's drawings. Of what it meant to lose and find again. She doesn't code it. She feels it.

The transmitter inhales.

Then—

—a sudden burst of heat.

The signal launches.

Silent. Invisible to most networks. But not all.

Far above, in orbiting satellites and deep-listening towers along Port Aurora, a dozen machines flicker in quiet alert.

And far away, somewhere inside a lonely console in IICHA's comms wing, a young tech murmurs: *"What the hell is that?"*

And deeper still—in the tangled traces of a PLA tactical array—another voice, cold and calculated, says:

"Confirm origin. Prepare retrieval."

But Aarya cannot hear them.

She feels only the calm that follows the act.

And something else.

A slow vibration under her skin.

A resonance rising from the soil beneath her feet—

—not danger. Not attack.

But answer.

The Grove is replying.

The pulse had been released—fanned through spores, laced in tremors, folded into low bioacoustic hums that carried across root and ruin. But it wasn't just a message. It was a form of remembering. Aarya crouched near the base of the central node, her palms buried in the loamy mesh, as if the act of grounding herself could stabilize what she'd just unleashed.

Then, the Grove stirred.

Not violently—but with intention.

The ambient light dimmed fractionally as mycelial fronds coiled, swayed, and shimmered in layered frequencies, each pulse meeting her spine with a subdermal whisper. She blinked, and across the space, points of soft luminescence aligned—like stars being mapped in motion.

The Grove was replying.

Not with words. Not with language. With impressions—dense packets of layered memory. The return signal, she realized, was not only bouncing back across the fungal lattice—but reconfiguring itself with her.

Her breath caught. Images flickered behind her eyes—not hallucinations, not fever dreams—but coded emotion. Rohan's voice, fragmented yet clear, tangled with her Baba's steady hands sketching spore patterns. Then Anjana's face. Her voice, clipped and urgent:

"Signal received. Attempting to locate origin. Aarya, is that you?"

The mycelium blinked again, absorbing and projecting.

"No... you're not just mirroring me," Aarya whispered, her voice cracking. *"You're choosing."*

The Grove had fused her message with their essence. The Gleamers' ecosystem wasn't just helping her reach out—it was deciding how much to let through. Which frequencies would be decipherable. Which would be protected. It was curating memory, selectively camouflaging itself inside her transmission.

Aarya stood, shakily. Somewhere beyond this forest, someone had heard her. Perhaps not the full story. But enough.

She had made contact.

And far away—deep in Port Aurora or maybe the high skies above Kolkata—someone was already moving toward her.

The signal had gone.

No fanfare, no blink of light. Just a hushed vibration through the spore threads, like a breath held and then released. Aarya sat motionless for a long while, her fingers still resting on the edge of the root-transistor, now dormant again. Outside, the sun was melting beyond the canopy, gilding the shack in a soft, clement bronze.

The Grove was still. Still in a way that felt like acknowledgment—not silence, but space. She stepped outside slowly, walking barefoot onto the mossy ridge that overlooked the southern rise. Her legs trembled, not with exhaustion but with a quiet reverence. She had done it.

The message now traveled—through wet networks, soundless and tangled, through airwaves laced with particulate language, through satellite drift and mycelial delay. Somewhere, someone would catch a whisper:

"It's not data—it's memory."

She leaned against the bamboo railing of the platform. From here, she could see the bay curl like a soft shell far below. The dark sea shimmered like a basin of mica. Somewhere out there, Rohan had once said, were the submerged ruins of a pre-colonial settlement, overgrown with coral and ignored by imperial maps. She smiled, as if the past had conspired to hide itself even from the future.

A flicker of green light at the edge of the trees caught her attention. She blinked. Another. Then another. Fireflies. But no—not quite. They pulsed in an odd pattern, a language she could nearly grasp. Her heart skipped.

The Grove was answering.

The night was warm and windless. The generator hum was off—Aarya had cut it hours ago. She sat on the floor of her shack, cross-legged, half-asleep and barefoot, letting the day's currents drift through her. A cup of cold, unsteeped tea sat forgotten beside her.

She felt them before she saw them.

A light shift in air pressure. A scent—petrichor and salt, but woven with an older musk, the perfume of spores and something almost metallic. Her eyes opened gently. She didn't flinch.

They stood at the threshold, silent, tall and slight and glowing faintly as if their bodies filtered moonlight through their bones. Five of them—maybe six. The edges of their forms blurred into the shack's shadows, like memories already half-departed.

Aarya rose slowly, her throat tight. Her breath came out soft:

"I didn't think you'd come."

No words were returned. But she felt them—soft pulses, an emotion that wasn't language but its ancestor. Gratitude. Sorrow. Something she couldn't name but understood. One of them, the smallest, stepped forward and pressed a hand— barely more than filaments wrapped in skin—against her wrist. It was warm.

The Grove outside seemed to pause, holding time in its fronds.

Aarya's voice cracked. *"You'll be safe now. I promise."*

They watched her, faces unreadable but kind. Then, without motion or drama, they turned, slipping out into the night like they had never arrived. No sound of footfall. No rustle in the ferns. Just their afterimage—like moonlight on water after a cloud passes.

Aarya stood alone once again, her hand tingling where she had been touched. Only much later, curled beneath the netting, her breath evening into sleep, did she whisper, *"Was that goodbye?"*

That night, she dreamed.

She stood not in the shack, but on the shore. Older, her hair streaked with grey, eyes gentle and firm. Rohan was beside her, weather-worn and smiling. They were visiting, not returning. A child played among the tidepools. The Grove watched from afar, distant but alive.

She awoke with a pang in her chest. She hadn't known, not fully—not until now.

They had come to say farewell.

***

Chapter 10 – The Return

South Veyra Shoreline | 17 April 2075 | 06:12 IST

The vessel broke the horizon just as the morning mist lifted. Sleek, white-bellied, and buzzing faintly above the waves, it glinted like a misplaced tooth in the untouched silence of the forest's edge. Aarya had known something was coming—she'd felt it in the mycelial tremors, in the way the air had been too still the past evening. But she hadn't expected it to arrive with this kind of stillness.

The Grove, as if understanding, had gone silent too. No flickering lights beneath the bark. No shimmering from the inner node. Just the breath of the sea and the chir of waking insects.

Atop the descending vessel, Anjana Bose's silhouette was unmistakable—leaning forward, wind-snapped hair, binoculars in hand. Behind her, a familiar stance, hand shielding his eyes, was Rohan.

Rohan.

Even from this distance, Aarya's breath caught. Not because she doubted he would come—but because the sight of him now, real and reaching, collapsed the thin barrier between all her past dreams and this moment. The fever-visions, the whispering spores, her longing for touch unmediated by code or fungus or memory—all of it rushed in.

She didn't move yet.

She let them land.

The vessel touched down with a careful hiss at the narrow clearing she had once marked unsafe for drones. Rohan jumped down first, scanning the tree line. Anjana followed, pulling out a small scanner. The rest of the crew held back, uncertain.

Then:

"Aarya!"

A pause.

"Aarya Sen, it's Anjana—We're here to take you home."

No one from the Grove stirred.

Aarya stepped forward.

But she did not yet answer.

Aarya stepped lightly, as if her feet might disturb the quiet pact of this soil. Every root beneath her felt like a thread tugged tight. She didn't run—she couldn't. The gravity of the moment was too dense for haste.

Rohan was already moving toward her, slowly, deliberately, as if approaching something fragile. His eyes locked onto hers—not searching, not doubting. Just there. Present.

They met halfway. The old way.

Not in words.

Just arms.

Wrapped, tight. Breaths uneven. Her forehead against his shoulder, her hands clutching his back as if afraid the world might pull her away before this was real.

"I thought I lost you," he whispered.

Aarya shook her head against him. *"I never left. Not really."*

From behind them, Anjana watched—shoulders slack, a relieved breath escaping her lips. She gave them a moment before approaching.

"We need to leave within the hour," she said gently. *"The PLA's surveillance net has expanded. They'll be sweeping this zone soon."*

"I know," Aarya replied, her voice quieter, tempered. *"I've already sent out the return signal."*

Rohan blinked. *"What return signal?"*

Aarya turned to him, a faint smile beneath tired eyes. *"One that says this place is far too complex to ever be colonized. A trap of memory, biology, and resistance. I wove it into the roots. The Grove helped."*

She glanced at the forest.

"They helped more than I deserved."

Just then, a breeze stirred the edges of the clearing—and for a flickering second, a shape shimmered between branches. Humanoid. Glowing faintly. Watching.

Rohan didn't see. But Anjana did.

She said nothing.

Neither did Aarya.

Because even goodbye, sometimes, must remain unseen.

Each step Aarya took on the moss-hushed path felt like walking backward through memory. Behind her, the Grove was still pulsing softly—its breath slow, like sleep, like mourning.

She had packed everything half an hour ago. The shack now stood empty, cleaned with care, as if she were returning it to something older than ownership. She left the sketch Baba had once made—of the spore bloom shaped like a listening ear—tucked beneath the floorboards.

The air was cool, touched by salt from the northern winds. Rohan walked a few paces behind, his presence respectful, wordless. He had seen her weep that morning, not loudly, but into her palms, like a prayer she couldn't finish.

She turned once.

The Grove, in the rising light, shimmered like it was already part of another world. Somewhere deep within, she thought she saw movement. A faint shape, not entirely human. Watching.

Not following.

"I'll come back," she whispered, though she knew they wouldn't hear it the way humans do.

No Gleamer had come to the edge.

She understood now that last night had been their farewell. Their silence now was not absence. It was ritual.

At the landing ridge, the makeshift transmitter she had built with the Grove's help still hummed in low cycles. It would loop memory, encoded in pulses and spores, long after she was gone.

Not a message of exposure. A message of refusal. Of wonder. Of warning.

A return signal in waiting.

Her boots crunched on the last stretch of gravel before the helipad. She paused once more, placing her hand on the trunk of a luminous lichen tree. It glowed faintly beneath her touch.

Rohan stepped beside her, quietly offering a canteen of water.

"Ready?" he asked.

Aarya nodded, not trusting her voice.

But the word she carried inside her chest wasn't 'yes.'

It was: Not yet.

And still, she walked.

The rotors gathered wind, shearing through the thick, luminous morning. As the helicopter lifted from the clearing, the ground unfurled beneath her—moss trails, fractured roots, the grove's half-hidden pulse shrinking into a patchwork of green and gold.

Aarya leaned toward the window. The horizon swayed as if reluctant to let her go. Through the plexiglass, the forest no longer rose to meet her but sank gently below, the canopy folding over secrets it had once offered up.

The first time she saw the island from above, it had felt like being pulled into a myth—an unnamed curve of earth and sea that refused translation. Now, as she departed, it looked smaller, contained—yet impossibly heavier, as if a thousand threads were still anchoring her heart beneath the canopy.

She didn't speak.

Rohan sat beside her, quiet, hands resting on his knees—his presence warm, steady. Anjana leaned slightly toward the front, coordinating with the IICHA pilot, her voice clipped but calm. No one asked Aarya if she was ready to leave.

Because she wasn't.

Aarya closed her eyes briefly. In her chest, the hum of the return signal still echoed—a living frequency stitched from Grove and grief, language and longing. Somewhere in the folds of fungal memory, she had left behind not just data, but devotion. And something—no, someone—had whispered back.

From above, the southern ridge vanished in mist. A trail of light bent across the ocean. The island did not wave. It did not mourn. But it remained—watching.

Aarya pressed her palm gently against the window, as if to touch it one last time.

And in that moment, she whispered not to Rohan, not to Anjana, but to the Grove itself:

"I will not forget."

Port Aurora Helipad, Andaman Base Sector | 17 April 2075 | 08:40 IST

The helipad shimmered with morning heat. Aarya stepped out, her boots meeting solid concrete after what felt like a lifetime suspended in breath and bioelectric memory. The salt in the air was sharper here, industrial, carrying not the warmth of spores but the steel tang of surveillance and structure.

Rohan followed, shielding his eyes from the sun. Anjana stepped ahead, speaking with a ground officer. For a moment, Aarya simply stood still, unsure which way to move, as if the soil beneath her had lost its pulse.

Then she saw Ma. She stood near the terminal gate—thin, composed, wearing the same sea-green shawl she always carried during uncertain weather. Her hair, streaked with grey, was pulled into a bun. Her eyes locked onto Aarya's, unblinking, as if afraid even the blink of a moment might lose her again.

Aarya's chest caught.

They said nothing. The space between them dissolved in three slow steps. Then, without warning, Aarya walked forward and wrapped her arms around her mother.

Paromita froze—then melted into the embrace, her hand rising hesitantly before pulling Aarya close, like she had done decades ago when the fever nightmares came.

"I'm sorry," Aarya whispered into her mother's shoulder.

"You came back," Paromita said. *"That's all that matters."*

The moment wasn't grand. It didn't need to be. Forgiveness, when it arrives, doesn't ask for ceremony. It only asks to be held.

Aarya stepped back, her eyes moist but steady. Paromita reached for her hand, and this time, Aarya didn't pull away.

Behind them, Rohan watched—his gaze softened, lips curved faintly upward. He didn't say anything. He didn't need to.

Anjana approached, nodding gently toward Paromita, then turned to Aarya with the warmest smile Aarya had seen from her. *"We'll talk. But not now. You're on leave,"* she said. *"For as long as you need. The rest can wait."*

The sun warmed Aarya's skin. The Grove was far behind—but not gone.

And just ahead, something else waited. Not a mission. Not a mystery.

Something like home.

THE END